LOVE WITHOUT RESERVATIONS

A Novel

Irene Williams

ISBN
978-1-7360803-2-0
978-1-7360803-3-7

Website:
Irenewilliamsbooks.com

Email:
Irenewill2020@gmail.com

Blessed is he whose transgression is forgiven,
whose sin is covered.

Psalm 32:1

ACKNOWLEDGEMENT

I have to give thanks to Jesus for providing me with another opportunity to publish my stories. I'd also like to thank Kim and Robert for the excellent editing work they've provided for this novel. To my family and friends: Clive, Jasmine, Chelsea, Khalia and Salvatore; I could not have completed this work without your encouragement, feedback and support.

LOVE
WITHOUT
RESERVATIONS

CHAPTER ONE
SHEPHERD'S BUSH

"Thank you so much for inviting me to your grand opening," said Simone.

"It was my pleasure to have you, and I appreciate all of the wonderful creative work you've done for my café. As you can see, it's being received well," said Kaleb, the shop's owner, as he escorted Simone to the door of his newly opened upscale coffee house, Jebena café.

During their initial meeting, Kaleb had explained how he used coffee beans harvested by female farmers who resided in small villages throughout his home province of Sidamo, Ethiopia, a region renowned for producing superior quality coffee beans. Kaleb had described how the women, who were taught from a young age how to harvest them, handpicked the beans in the forest.

After her first meeting with Kaleb, Simone had thought it would be great to tell his customers where their coffee came from, and who they were supporting. She'd designed an interior collage wall that depicted the process of the arabica coffee development cycle. It began with photos of the female Sidamo farmers harvesting and sorting the beans, then continued with pictures of the beans being transported, processed with temperature control, and packaged. The bottom of the collage, which was at eye level, displayed individual pictures of these women with a small biography for each.

She'd also used an illustration of a young green arabica plant seedling held in the palm of a hand as the logo for Kaleb's business. The former accountant turned shop owner had immediately loved the logo design because he believed it portrayed the ambiance he wanted for his establishment. The logo now adorned his shop displays, cups, and merchandise.

His café's grand opening had had a terrific turnout; Kaleb and his barista had distributed free coffee samples, poured from their traditional Ethiopian Jebena Clay brewing pots into newly designed recyclable cups embossed with his logo. The shop saw a steady stream of traffic until late in the day, with many purchasing the baked goods he also sold.

Simone was elated; it was a wonderful feeling to have her work appreciated by the client *and* his customers. Though her business was still new and in need of much nurturing, she could sense that her hard work and sacrifice were starting to pay off. She felt as though her design and photography business was beginning to move in the right direction.

Simone had long ago determined to be a sole proprietor at some point in her career. She'd never planned specifically to do this in England, it had just worked out that way. Opening a business in another country was no easy task; the first few months were scary, and hardly anyone had walked into her studio; but those days were behind her now.

Kaleb's grand opening capped a long, exhausting day for Simone. Tomorrow's schedule included a photo shoot for a wine seller who wanted professional photos for his website, and meetings with two couples in need of a wedding photographer. The first couple had booked an appointment because of a personal recommendation; they were already familiar with her work and were ready to make arrangements. The second couple had made an appointment when they came across her website. They loved what they'd seen of her work, but were hesitant about her prices. Simone was confident in the price she'd quoted for the couple's destination wedding as it was located over 100 miles outside of London. She'd calculated the cost of her driving time into the final figure, so there was no getting around the expense. The young designer/photographer had known when she started her business that a car was needed to reach certain locations and to carry her equipment. But England's petrol costs were astronomical compared to the US and her business could not support the cost of purchasing a new car; so, for now, her leased blue Vauxhall was all she could afford.

Walking to her car made Simone painfully aware that she'd been on her feet for over fourteen hours. Once inside, Simone closed her eyes for a few minutes before starting the vehicle; she couldn't wait to go home and crawl into bed. The fact that her home was also her place of business was a definite plus; not having to commute to work to open her shop at 9 AM was wonderful.

The streets remained damp from the light drizzle of rain that had turned off and on throughout the day. After five years of living in London, Simone was confident driving the showery London streets. Listening to the GPS dictate directions, she drove her Vauxhall assuredly through the Shepherd's Bush community, a trendy location with an active nightlife. Abruptly, the light drizzle turned into a downpour, forcing Simone to drive slower and increase her wiper speed. The sparsely inhabited streets emptied as the torrential rain soaked the sidewalks, and it became difficult for Simone to see the street signs.

When the small car turned the corner onto a narrow road,

she viewed what appeared to be a roadblock, except with camera flashes. Cars in front of her were blowing their horns in protest to the blockage. As she inched closer, Simone realized the roadblock was actually a group of paparazzi. Simone blew her horn but they barely reacted to her presence as they continued to flash their cameras in the direction of a small grey Porsche with tinted windows. Simone looked up and noted that this street ran behind what appeared to be an arena or theatre.

The paparazzi were blocking the car in while the driver blew their horn repeatedly, with no response from the photographers. Simone felt so sorry for the poor soul trapped in their own car with no escape. She continued to blow her horn but the spectators weren't moving. A glance in the rearview mirror confirmed that there was no way to back up because other cars were behind her now.

Simone rolled down the window and yelled, "How many pictures do you need to take!" In response, one photographer turned and gave her a two fingered V sign. That was it, she'd had enough! Simone yelled, "Please move out of the way! You are blocking traffic!" Some of them moved, but another banged on her car as she inched forward. Now she was furious. A few more minutes passed and she couldn't take it anymore. Simone revved her car and drove as if she were going to run them over. They shouted at her; some banged her car with their hands, but they began to slowly move out of her way.

She inched further down the street and peered into the grey sports car. It looked like the driver was on their phone, probably calling the authorities for help. She felt sorry for whoever it was and wanted to help, but how? The paparazzi were still shouting at her and it was complete chaos. That's when she got a crazy idea! As she inched forward, Simone brought the vehicle closer to the sports car. She wound down her window and could see two people in the car, so she waved her hands at the Porsche window to get their attention. When a window lowered, Simone yelled, "Get into my back seat!" Without missing a beat, the driver and passenger quickly jumped into her back seat. The paparazzi were clearly furious at the interruption, and started banging on her car again, but Simone only drove more aggressively so they had no choice but to move out of her way. When her car cleared the mob, Simone sped off.

"Thank you miss; they kept us trapped forever," she heard from her back seat.

"I can't believe what they were doing to you. Why were they hounding you so much?" asked Simone.

"Well, as we were leaving the venue, my friend here got into a verbal altercation with one of the photographers who refused to move out of his way. When they started arguing, all the others descended on us like vultures; there were cameras everywhere."

"I was trying to avoid trouble but the one bloke kept sticking his camera directly in my face. He was so close I smell his breath," said the second passenger.

"There must have been a lot going on in this venue for so many photographers to appear. Was there some special artist appearing tonight or something?" asked Simone. There was a strange silence from the back seat while Simone waited for a reply. It dawned on her then that she had just picked up two strange men on a late rainy night. Simone felt the hairs on the back of her neck begin to rise and fearful thoughts came to her mind.

She asked, "Would you guys like me to drop you off at the Royal Garden Hotel, there should be taxis there and it's not far away?"

"That would be great miss, we would appreciate that," said the first passenger.

Great, she thought as she took short glances at her back seat. It was dark but there was something familiar about the two men. Simone decided to engage them in small talk.

"What do you two do, if you don't mind my asking?"

The first passenger stated, "We're musicians."

The second passenger asked, "What type of work do you do miss?"

"I'm a designer and photographer," she said.

"You have a nice Yankee accent, have you been here long from the States?" he asked.

Simone told them she was originally from New York, specifically Brooklyn, but had finished her art degree in London a few years ago and decided to stay and open her own business. She went in depth about the type of work she did and promised to give them cards when she reached the hotel. The second passenger seemed very interested; she wondered if he could be a potential client, because you never knew.

The interested party asked more questions about her work, so Simone discussed her interest in portrait painting, but the conversation was cut short when they reached the hotel. Several taxis were parked in front of the hotel entrance when Simone pulled over to the curb and stopped the car. Her passengers thanked her profusely and stepped out, the second one trying to give her money. Simone turned it down, telling him it was her good deed for the day. That's when he stooped down to her open window and held out his hand to shake hers. Though the rain continued to pour, she could see him clearly, and suddenly realized who he was! Simone was having a conversation with Thomas Lloyd.

Her heart started pounding as she shook his hand. Simone peered at the other passenger and recognized him as the guitarist from the band Thomas Lloyd was part of, Alistair Simmons. Alistair had his signature blonde dreads pulled back into a pony tail. Realizing she was still clutching Thomas's hand, she quickly released it.

"Are you certain I can't offer you any money?" Thomas asked again. Simone was overwhelmed and speechless but managed to shake her head no.

He took out a card. "Just in case you change your mind," he said. Thomas then wrote his cell number on the back and handed it to her.

"Thank you" was all she could say.

"Ah, I believe you promised me your card," he said.

"Oh sorry, I forgot." Simone fumbled in her handbag and pulled out several cards to give him.

"Thank you again Simone," he said with a huge smile as he took the cards from her hand. She watched the two as they walked to a taxi. Realizing she held her breath, Simone exhaled. She could not believe that she'd been having casual conversation in her car with Thomas Lloyd, the lead singer of the Access band. How could she not have known? Alistair with his hair pulled back could have been anyone, and Thomas's short spiked hair made him look more like Adam Levine than his usual shoulder-length haired self. Truth was, it was so dark and unexpected, she never would have guessed who they were.

Simone remembered how well-liked Access was when they toured the US years ago. Their music was very popular when she was in high school, and Thomas's face was on the cover of many magazines. Now in his early forties, the short-cropped hair was sprinkled with a few greys, and the medium-sized mustache made him look like a different person; but he was still very attractive. Not rail thin as he was in his early years; now, Thomas wore a slightly stockier build.

Simone closed her eyes and thought of his smile. Then,

bringing herself back to reality, she put her car into gear and started home.

It was a little before eleven when she parked in front of her studio; too late to call her friend Nikki to tell her all about her exciting experience. Instead, she took a shower and tried to get some sleep.

CHAPTER TWO
THE MILLS FAMILY HISTORY

Robert and Laura Mills surprised their little girl with a small paint set for Christmas when she was four. They'd seen how much she enjoyed painting in preschool, and they wanted to give their creative daughter something she would enjoy. At preschool, the couple thought Simone's paintings looked much better than the other kids', but they were her parents, and weren't sure if they were only seeing what they wanted to. Throughout the Christmas school break, Simone stayed in her room, painting nonstop. Her parents checked on her often, and sometimes found her fast asleep with the brush still clutched in her hand. From that Christmas on, the four-year-old, who already loved painting portraits, decided that she wanted to be an artist when she grew up.

During Simone's early teen years, Robert and Laura Mills's marriage fell apart. The divorce finalized after Simone's college preparatory tests were completed. The years the Mills's transitioned from a loving family of four into a complete mess were difficult times for Simone and her older brother, Martin.

The divorce wasn't a shock. In Simone's mind, her parents separated a long time before it became official, and were just going through the motions of marriage; there was no warmth between them.

Even after the divorce, their family dynamics were still messy as far as Simone was concerned. Returning home for the holidays often created a dilemma. She wanted to stay with her mother in their New York home but her father, who had moved to Florida with his girlfriend, Cindy, after Simone graduated from high school, always asked her to spend time with him. Last year, she spent Thanksgiving with her mother and Christmas with her father and Cindy in Boca Raton. Her brother, who'd already finished college and resided in Maryland with his girlfriend, would drive up to spend time with their mother, but never visited their father in Florida.

Simone felt sorry that her mother had to live alone but she didn't place all the blame for the divorce on her dad. In fact, she viewed Laura's attitude as the primary cause of the divorce. Her mother was a controlling and rigid wife who never compromised during disagreements. Simone's passive father had always allowed Laura to dictate all matters that concerned the household. To outsiders, they were the perfect nuclear family; however, Simone and Martin knew better.

Robert Mills committed the ultimate marital crime; he cheated on his wife—and not just one time. Robert Mills had an ongoing secret affair with his coworker. He was happy to keep their little secret separate from his family, but Cindy had other ideas. Ideas she didn't discuss with Robert until it was too late.

One day, Cindy showed up on Laura's doorstep with information that ripped the Mills family apart. Laura, hurt and disappointed, responded with rage and vicious revenge. *Angry* was too simple a word to describe the emotions and actions Laura displayed. First, she tried to obtain full control of all their present and future assets; then, Laura decided not to hide her husband's infidelity. She told the world, calling every family member and friend who would listen to report all the details Cindy had shared with her. Laura wanted Robert's integrity and reputation to be dirt.

At the time of their parents' separation, Martin was living in Maryland; Simone wasn't as fortunate. She had no choice but to hear and see it all; the arguments, the crying, the screaming. The young teen hated what her father did—she was ashamed of him—but having to listen to her mother tear down his character every day made her want to be anywhere but home.

Custody arrangements required that she spend Easter and summer breaks with her father in Florida. In the beginning, Simone disliked Cindy and hated having to share her father with her on visits; she was his little girl and she missed her dad. Still wanting to keep a close relationship with her dad, Simone called him often from school or home; and Robert would always pass the phone to Cindy for Simone to say hello. He wanted his daughter and his girlfriend to develop a cordial relationship; however, it irritated Simone that she was forced to talk to Cindy. Truthfully, she felt strange asking how Cindy was doing because she honestly didn't care. How could she care for the woman who'd seduced her father and destroyed her family? Simone saw Cindy as the cause of her weakening relationship with her father and the cause of her mother's tears. There would never be a good relationship between herself and Cindy, but for her father's sake, she forced herself to be tolerant.

Through it all, Simone never lost sight of her goal to become an artist. She was accepted to Gramercy Arts High School in Manhattan where she learned many forms of artistic expression; studying photography, website design, and chorus. From there, she studied arts at St. Vincent College in Syracuse for her bachelor's degree. Simone further distanced herself from her father after she went away to college. It became Robert who tried to stay in touch with his daughter, though she rarely called or returned his calls.

Thinking about all the obstacles she overcame in her past made Simone proud of her business. Owning her own company was a dream she'd had since high school. She wasn't sure why, maybe it was the desire to be in control of her career. The original plan was to open a business in Brooklyn after receiving her graduate degree. Simone even came up with the company name, Brooklyn Graphics, during her junior year of high school.

That plan was upended when she won a full scholarship to attend The Royal College of Art in London. The scholarship severed her financial dependence on her parents. The Mills's, however, weren't concerned about financing, they disliked the idea of their daughter living so far away from them. Unfazed by her parent's fears, Simone jumped at the opportunity she'd been presented and moved to London even sooner than planned.

The cultural differences took some getting used to, but once she'd gotten her bearings, Simone thrived. She quickly obtained a salaried graphic arts internship and worked after her classes. The money helped her to save for her goal. After working four years, Simone qualified to apply for permanent residency, and the residency status placed her in a better position to open Brooklyn Graphics in London.

Obtaining the shop's financing was tougher than Simone had expected. The process was long and tedious, with many disappointing rejections to her loan requests. Limited cash flow, or rather, lack of adequate cash flow, was a serious impediment to receiving approval. Though many financiers praised her business plan, her loan approval didn't arrive until the last minute. Simone was proud of herself; at the age of twenty-six she'd accomplished her goal of opening her own business. Her company, Brooklyn Graphics, had to take on more services than she'd originally planned to offer, such as selling print artwork to supplement revenue, but in the end, it was all hers.

Doing things at the right time was one of those lessons the novice business owner had had to learn. Brooklyn Graphics opened for business on December 15TH. Unlike America, British businesses wind down and prepare for the Christmas holiday season, and Simone did not make substantial commercial sales until the following spring.

Simone had anticipated her family's negative reaction to her opening a business in London; so, she didn't mention her business plan until her loan and rental space were secured. Even then, eager to convince their little girl to change her mind, Simone's parents had promised to pull money out of their retirement funds to cover her business loan debts if she would return to New York. Martin came over to visit, but as she suspected, he was sent by Robert and Laura to convince her to return to New York. As part of his tactics, Martin expressed concern at her leaving their mother all alone, but Simone reminded him that their mother had been alone for several years and never complained about it.

Simone loved working in London, but the dream of painting portraits never materialized. The American figured British people would be more receptive to portraiture, but though there's a tremendous amount of portrait art history appreciation in the British Isles, there were no responses to her portrait painting offers. As portraiture became relegated to a hobby, Simone made her friends Nikki and Derrick pose for paintings in their free time. She hung their portraits alongside her favorite landscape paintings of Bermuda, which she'd completed during the Mills's last vacation as a family. As commercial design and website orders increased, Simone's portrait dream diminished.

CHAPTER THREE
DERRICK & NIKKI

In the morning, Simone jumped out of bed and rushed to the bathroom. All she could think of was calling Nikki to tell her all about last night. After dressing, she quickly whipped up a batch of muffins and threw them in the oven. Leaving the kitchen, she entered her studio to do some minor cleaning before unlocking the door for customers. With her chores done, she sat down and dialed Nikki. The time was 9:05; Nikki arrived at work by 8 AM, but for some reason Simone's call was going to voicemail.

When the bell on her studio door rang, Simone pressed the buzzer to let Derrick in. He held the usual, two steaming cups of coffee.

"Good morning Derrick," Simone said cheerfully, "I'll be right back." This was part of their Friday morning ritual: Derrick, who lived next door, would bring two cups of coffee to Simone's shop after his assistant arrived to cover the desk at his travel agency next door, and Simone would always have some baked goods on hand.

Looking at him, one would never think of Derrick as a man who liked baked goods. At six foot three, the thirty-year-old Scandinavian-looking blond had muscles that left no doubt that he was into body building. Derrick worked out several days a week and played in the community rugby club, but he wasn't your typical fitness addict; Derrick was a master of his finances. In addition to Simone's space, Derrick Manning owned a row of storefront properties that he'd inherited from his late father. Charles Manning's first property was the Manning Travel Agency, an agency so successful it had allowed Charles to purchase all the surrounding properties on his street.

It was Nikki who'd told Simone about the commercial properties her cousin Derrick managed. When they met, he gave Simone historical data about the previous businesses that had occupied the space she was viewing. In his office, Derrick showed Simone a well-organized binder filled with community demographics and lifestyle information about the neighborhood. He provided Simone with specific information, like the count for the number of people who walked past the space every day, the closest forms of mass transportation, and the complete census for the suburb of Acton, London. She knew from her search that the lessee normally had to research this information on their own, so Simone was very appreciative of Derrick's organization.

Their ritual began before Simone's grand opening of Brooklyn Graphics. The opening was on a Friday; that morning, Derrick welcomed her with a fresh-brewed cup of coffee. Simone had made fresh chocolate chip cookies for the walk-in customers and placed them on the counter. Together, they enjoyed the coffee and, surprisingly to Simone, Derrick helped himself to several cookies.

Acton wasn't congested like central London, but it possessed a good mix of pedestrian and business traffic. Once she opened for business, Simone received many walk-in clients from the neighborhood. Most of her residential customers came for wedding and special occasion photography. The commercial clients were where Simone focused most of her creative energies; they were mainly sole proprietors like herself. She tried her best to give cost breaks to new startups because she knew firsthand the difficulties of starting a business in London.

That morning, Simone reentered the studio carrying a tray of the warm muffins she'd removed from the oven a few minutes ago.

Simone loved to bake, but there's no fun in eating your baked foods by yourself. If it weren't for Derrick and Nikki, she'd probably have stopped baking altogether. Instead, today she'd made sweet corn muffins, one of Derrick's new favorites. He'd never eaten cornbread before she'd offered him the muffins, as it's not as popular in England as in the US. Last week she made soft raisin cinnamon pretzels. Derrick had looked at them strangely but once he'd bitten into one of the soft buttery pretzels, he'd added it to the top of his list of favorites. Simone enjoyed introducing her new friends to her favorite foods; they'd loved everything she'd made so far.

The love of baking was passed onto her from her paternal grandmother, whom she called Nanna. The Mills siblings spent many summer breaks with their Carolinian grandmother—who Simone remembered had always smelled of lavender—because Nanna took care of them until school was back in session. Simone's mother had always said that Simone had taken on her grandmother's personality.

The stimulating coffee was just what she needed this morning. Simone couldn't shake last night's events from her thoughts, and she'd tossed and turned the remainder of the night instead of sleeping. Though she valued him as a good friend and conversationalist, Derrick was a known gossip, so there was no way she'd trust Derrick to keep her information to himself; Nikki was her only safe option.

"So, how was the opening? You got in pretty late last night," said Derrick.

"It went extremely well; Kaleb was very pleased. I left after nine, and he still had quite a few customers; the free coffee samples helped a great deal. It was pouring rain when I got to my car and I had to give a few people a lift, but I'm glad I went," she said.

"Who did you give a lift to so late at night? Was it someone you knew?" Derrick asked. Simone wished she could kick herself for letting that information slip.

"Um, no, I didn't know them well, but they were nice enough. I dropped them off at a hotel. You know, someone asked about your rental unit the other day. I told your assistant about it; did you get a chance to speak to them?"

"I've been meaning to call them; unfortunately the flat is still occupied. I have to do something about Ms. Davies; she was to move out three weeks ago, but she hasn't budged. Her furniture is still inside and she refuses to let me show the apartment when she's not there. I hate to badger people but I feel she's taking the piss. The lease finished a month ago. I've asked her every week when she's going to move; she keeps promising to move on the weekend, yet she's still here. She's promised to pay for each week she's stayed past the lease date, but I haven't seen any money yet," Derrick complained.

"Oh well, I'm sure she'll make a move eventually and she still has her job, so hopefully some payment is coming your way," said Simone.

"People having a job doesn't mean they take care of their responsibilities. You'd be amazed how many people waste their rent money on the pub or on an expensive coat, then turn to the landlord and say they don't have any rent money," said Derrick.

Simone's cell phone rang; it was Nikki. "*Hey Simone, were you trying to reach me? My manager grabbed me for another unplanned morning meeting as soon as I walked in the door. We've just wrapped up so I have a few minutes now,*" she said.

"Excuse me Derrick; I'll be right back. I have to take this call," said Simone.

"Oh, don't worry, I might as well get back to my office now. See you in a bit," he said as he walked off. Simone waved him off, then got back to Nikki.

"Nikki, are you sitting down?!" she said with excitement.

"*Yes, my goodness, you sound so pumped, which is very unusual for you. Is Derrick there?*"

"No, he just left. I have some very exciting news to tell you!"

"*Simone, tell me already, I can hear the excitement in your voice. What happened?*"

"Well, you remember the event I went to last night? After leaving I did something I never thought I would ever do. As I was driving through Shepherd's Bush, I turned the corner to drive down this narrow road but I couldn't get through because throngs of paparazzi were hounding this little sports car that was parked on the street, which is in the back of an arena. I honked the horn and yelled at them but they wouldn't budge, so I started inching my car into them and, in the spur of the moment, I got the idea to rescue their victims. I pulled up to the sports car and told the driver to get into my back seat. After they got in I left as fast as I could. You'll never guess who my passengers were!"

"*OMG, it was you! No, I can't believe you did that,*" said Nikki.

Simone was confused. "What do you mean by `it was you'? I haven't finished telling you the story."

"Oh Simone, you don't know?" said Nikki.

"Know what?" said Simone.

"Simone, did you see the Daily Mail this morning? I'm looking at it again now and I just realized it's a photo of your car in the article. The headline says, 'Tom's mysterious gal pal rescues him from…"

Simone quickly grabbed the newspaper Derrick had left behind and looked for the article.

"Oh no, Nikki, what have I done? How did this happen? I was just trying to help them out. This is insane!"

"Simone calm down, it's OK. They're not showing you or your license plate; I wouldn't worry about it. But I can't believe you gave Thomas Lloyd a ride in your car. Why didn't you make me come with you to the opening? What did he say to you? How did he look? Did you take a selfie with him? I would never have thought you *would do such a thing,"* said Nikki, all without taking a breath.

"I can't believe I did it either; I never pick up strangers. I just felt sorry for whoever was trapped in the car, and I was upset because the road was blocked. Oh, I almost forgot! Thomas gave me his card and wrote his number on it."

"Shut up!" shouted Nikki. *"You have his personal cell number! You should have called me the second you got in last night,"* said Nikki.

"It was very late; you were definitely already in bed," said Simone.

"I would have happily woken up for this info. When are you going to call him?" asked Nikki.

"I'm not going to call him; he gave me the card in case I changed my mind about accepting money for the ride I gave them. I've already said that he didn't have to pay me."

"We will have to discuss this in depth later; I've got to get back to work now. Are you still making me dinner tonight?"

"Yes, I'll see you at six; give me a buzz if you think you'll be late." Just as Simone put her cell phone down, her work phone started to ring. She picked it up and answered, "Brooklyn Graphics, may I help you?"

"Hello Simone, is that you?" asked a voice that sounded a lot like the Thomas she'd met last night.

"Oh, hi…Thomas? It's nice of you to call."

"I hope I didn't call at a bad time; I just wanted to phone and apologize for getting your vehicle on the front pages of the tabloids. It's not fair—you did a good deed for us and your reward was to wake up to the rags talking about you," said Thomas.

"Please don't worry about it, I'm sure they'll have someone new to talk about tomorrow. But it was so nice of you to call, thank you."

"Well, the thing is, I feel very bad about putting you in that situation. I want to make it up to you somehow; so, I was wondering if you'd at least let me take you to lunch. Please say yes, it will make me feel much better. Would you be available this Sunday?"

"Yes, that sounds great; I'd love to go to lunch, but Sunday may not be the best time. I won't leave church until about 12:30 and it may take a while for me to reach the restaurant because my church is an hour outside the city," said Simone.

"I'll tell you what, why don't I have my driver pick you up from your home. He will take you back when we're done so you don't have to worry about driving. Should I have him pick you up at two?"

Wow, a driver, Simone thought. "Yes, two o'clock will be fine. How should I dress?" she asked.

"Wear whatever you're comfortable in; the place is very casual."

"Great, that sounds like a plan. Thank you so much,

Thomas, you can send your driver to the address on the card," said Simone.

"*Wonderful, I'll see you Sunday afternoon then,*" he said. Simone hung up the phone and exhaled with a smile. She couldn't believe she would be having lunch with Thomas Lloyd.

****

Nikki arrived for dinner at six with a bottle of sauvignon blanc for their meal. Simone had prepared shrimp burritos, using herbs freshly cut from her small garden. She enjoyed having fresh herbs to toss into her meals mere minutes after they've been cut and washed.

"Dinner was lovely, Simone. Next Friday it's my turn. Now, let's get to the good stuff! I want to know everything; you can start with what Thomas was wearing," Nikki told her.

"To be honest, I didn't notice what he was wearing. It was pouring rain and he stood in it, waiting for me to shake his hand. I was so mesmerized by his calm smile; it was genuinely sweet. I remember just staring at him like an idiot until he asked for my card. Before we go any further, I have to tell you about his call this morning, said Simone.

Nikki gasped, "He called?"

"Yes, he reached out to apologize for pictures of my car being plastered in the tabloids, and he's taking me out to lunch on Sunday to make up for it. He's even sending his driver to pick me up," said Simone with a smile.

"Oh, you are the luckiest girl in London! Where's he taking you?"

"I'm not sure. He didn't say, but he did say to dress casually."

"Hmm, we will have to sort through your utilitarian wardrobe to find something appropriate to wear. Wait, I have a better idea. We'll go shopping in the morning. You haven't shopped in a while and I believe you're long overdue," said Nikki.

"Nikki, what are you trying to say?"

"I'm not *trying* to say it. I *am* saying you need to add life to your dead wardrobe. If your clothes could speak, they would say, 'I'm all-business-and-no-fun Simone.'"

"Well, if you really think my clothes are that bad, I'll go just this once."

"This is interesting. I've been trying to take you shopping for the past year, and all I've heard from you is excuses, but when Thomas Lloyd gives you one smile, you're ready to go without me having to twist your arm. That must have been some smile," Nikki teased.

After Nikki left, Simone called her mother. Thanksgiving holiday was coming up and she'd originally intended to spend it with her mother at their home in Brooklyn, but she'd been thinking and had decided that her business needed as much revenue as possible before the Christmas holiday season. Based on last December's sales, Simone knew the upcoming twelfth month's sales would be uncertain, so she was now planning to go home the day before Christmas Eve and return the first week in January. Laura was upset because it would be the first time Simone wouldn't be with her family for Thanksgiving. Feeling guilty, Simone promised that next year would be different (though she wasn't confident she could keep her promise).

****

Simone had no plans for a huge shopping spree; nevertheless, even she had to admit that her wardrobe was in dire need of refreshment. Plus, Nikki was the best shopping companion a person could get; besides being a junior designer for a top advertising agency, Nikki was an avid discount fashionista, and knew the location of every designer bargain rack in London.

As the two friends entered their third store, Nikki found the perfect fitted sweater dress for her single twenty-six-year-old friend. It was a cashmere eggplant-purple knitted dress with hints of grey metallic threading throughout. Simone's normal dress size was US size four; however, she selected a size up because she felt the dress clung too well to her curvy backside. Nikki protested, swearing the larger dress sagged in places it shouldn't, but Simone wouldn't allow her friend to switch it back to the size four.

Nikki paired the dress with high heeled black booties and a conservative black leather moto jacket. After the purchases were made, Nikki dragged Simone to the salon to have the split ends trimmed off her long auburn hair. Simone didn't mind; she had planned to get a haircut ages ago as her mane almost reached her waist. Not completely satisfied, Nikki then coaxed her friend into an exfoliating facial, and she made Simone purchase updated eye shadow colors that she knew would accentuate Simone's green eyes.

"That's it, I'm not getting my nails done. I like them at their natural length. Besides, this is not a date, it's only a `thank you' lunch. We'll have a little polite conversation, maybe I'll take a couple of selfies with him, and then I'm coming home," said Simone.

"Simone, I'm trying to help you out. Just trust me, you'll thank me later. I know it's not a date but it's the closest thing to a real date that you've had since we graduated," said Nikki.

"That's not true, I've dated Oliver from the London Artist Association and I've dated Mark from church."

"Simone, Oliver doesn't count. Remember, you walked out on him when he told you he was polyamorous. And you told me that Mark was nice but that having conversation with him was too much work. Listen, your boat's been dry docked for too long. It's time to take it for a little cruise, time to put your oars in the water. I'm sure your church friends must wonder why a pretty girl like you is still single," said Nikki.

"You leave them out of it; you're the only one who thinks like this. These days, my focus has to stay on my business. I promise to put dating on my priority list after my revenue stabilizes. And just why haven't you been on a date lately?" asked Simone.

"I am trying to remedy that situation. I haven't been able to hook any big fish like you, but my day will come," said Nikki.

Exasperated, Simone reminded Nikki again that this was not a date, though she was looking forward to the lunch and hoped there was a possibility they could become friends.

CHAPTER FOUR
UNIVERSITY

The acceptance letter to her first-choice university was all Simone could think about during her senior year of high school. Going away to college meant independence; it meant she could do whatever she wanted to do.

Ultimately, Simone was admitted to the prestigious Saint Vincent University in Syracuse, New York, with a fifty percent tuition merit scholarship. Both parents were very proud of her accomplishment, but they cringed at the thought of their Simi being so far from family. Simone, like her brother, Martin, looked forward to going away to college.

However, the excitement waned after she moved into her dormitory. Simone couldn't help but long for the comforts of her Brooklyn home life where Laura worked evenings as a registered nurse, which meant her mother would always be home when Simone returned from school. Dinner would be waiting when she stepped in the door. All Simone had to do was study and keep her room clean.

The college meals served in the cafeteria were not up to her standards. All the meats were fried; the salads were withered and stale. Students weren't allowed to cook in their dorm areas, but there were kitchens on each floor for those students who preferred to make their own meals. Simone kept her small refrigerator well stocked; and though preparing her own meals was a chore, she had no appetite for the cafeteria foods or the fast-food restaurants near the campus, so it was a necessity.

Three other freshmen women resided in the quad dorm room alongside Simone. Each had her own bed and personal space, but little privacy. The common area remained unkept as all dorm mates were obviously used to someone else cleaning up after them.

Sandy was a tough, 5' 9", combat-boot-wearing brunette from Boston who always smelled of cannabis. Like Simone, Norma was from New York City. She had short black hair and a petite build similar to Simone's. She was a nice girl, but Simone was certain Norma was bulimic; the bathroom always smelled of vomit when she exited. Lisa was an average-sized blonde who seemed normal. Though she was from the local Syracuse area, she'd opted to live on campus. Lisa was the only roommate who had a boyfriend. When a visitor knocked, it was usually Lisa's boyfriend, Matt. Simone didn't like Matt spending so much time in their room, but she didn't want to be the only one to complain. His presence irritated her because she often caught him watching her. Generally, the roommates were polite to each other, but everyone kept to themselves and there was no real bonding; at least nothing like what you'd see in the movies.

Though each had her own refrigerator, occasionally one would help herself to Simone's food or use her milk without asking. She could never find out who it was, so she'd taped a "private, do not touch" sign to her refrigerator. But whoever it was generally ignored the sign, helping themselves to whatever they wanted without any regard for her personal privacy.

"Has anyone been in my refrigerator?" Simone asked angrily one day when she discovered more of her items missing. Again, all parties denied taking anything from it. Simone poured out her milk because she wasn't sure if the thief drank from the carton. Fed up over the secret thievery, she decided to catch the crook by setting a food trap. The next Sunday she baked a batch of chocolate brownies in the kitchen. When the brownies were done, she microwaved chocolate laxative pieces, melting them into a chocolate frosting before smearing it all over the top of the brownies. The brownies were left in a bag marked, "DO NOT EAT MY BROWNIES!"

Simone attended her Monday classes as usual. When she returned to the room and checked her refrigerator, half of the brownies were missing. It didn't take long to figure out who the perpetrator was. It wasn't the cannabis smoker or the bulimic. Lisa was going to the bathroom repeatedly. Initially, Simone felt victorious, but then Lisa left the bathroom when she should have stayed. The next rush visit to the toilet ended badly because it was occupied, and Lisa came back into the room crying because she'd messed herself. Simone and the other roommates helped her to get back in the bathroom with a change of clothing. Feeling guilty, Simone brought her a bottled water, afraid the girl would become dehydrated. Afterwards, she went back to her refrigerator and threw out the remaining brownies. The next day, Simone was summoned from one of her classes into the dean's office.

"Ms. Mills, you are here because your roommate Lisa Stannic reported your actions to me. She said you gave her brownies with the intention of making her ill," he stated. Simone couldn't believe what was happening; Lisa had stolen her food and then wanted *her* to be penalized for her theft?

Simone thought, *this is ridiculous, I don't understand why Lisa is lying.* She was about to defend herself by telling the dean about the trap she'd set, but before she could, she remembered how she'd heard about people losing their scholarships over silly things like what she'd done. Simone didn't want to be a member of that group, so she replied, "What brownies? I don't have any brownies."

The dean decided to do a little investigating, and came to their room and asked Sandy and Norma if Simone had offered them brownies; they both said no. The dean opened Simone's mini fridge and searched thoroughly but found nothing. The matter was dropped and Simone was permitted to return to class. Simone was free, but she'd made an enemy; Lisa remained combative and spiteful towards her for the rest of the semester.

Simone had told her brother what happened, and though he reprimanded her for setting the food trap, he'd also shipped her a refrigerator lock and advised her to apply for a room change. Unfortunately, the housing department didn't have any unoccupied rooms.

****

Though dorm life was disappointing, the freshman enjoyed her first college photography class; it was her favorite course thus far. All the students enjoyed Professor Henri Janssen's style of teaching; it was fresh and unconventional. The well-known published photographer from Amsterdam had opened Simone's mind to concepts of photography she'd never thought of. She was especially intrigued with mixed media photography and spent many hours of her free time working on this process for her projects. Professor Janssen frequently commented on her skills, and on many occasions he referred to her work as "gifted." After one class in particular, the professor asked if Simone was interested in helping him work on a new mixed media project.

"It would be a great privilege for me to work with you, Professor Janssen," replied Simone.

"Great, it would help me a great deal. Would you be able to come to my loft at 4 PM on Saturday? Let me write down the address. Don't bring your camera, I have all the equipment we need there," said the professor.

Simone couldn't belief her luck. How many freshmen had been given the opportunity to work on a project with their favorite professor? Saturday couldn't come soon enough, though Simone prepared in the meantime by going over all her notes on mixed media photography to ensure she didn't disappoint the professor.

The loft was a twenty-minute walk from her campus dormitory, and she arrived early, hoping that Professor Janssen would see that she was serious about working on the project. He greeted her warmly after he opened the door. Dressed in jeans and a T-shirt instead of his usual suit, he looked more like an older graduate student than a seasoned professor. They sat down and discussed the project in depth before he brought Simone to his art studio. The project would incorporate paints applied delicately to an assortment of blurred enlarged digital photographs printed on special watercolor paper. Once Simone was clear on their path, they got to work immediately and time went by quickly.

During a break, Professor Janssen ordered a pizza for them, then asked, "So, Simone, tell me about yourself. Where are you from originally?"

Simone started talking about her art studies in high school. The professor asked about her family and home life, and she found she was happy to talk about her home. She went into detail, describing her family, and even her parents' divorce. After they finished their pizza, Professor Janssen suggested she go home before it got too dark outside. He then asked if she would have any time to spare on Sunday. She quickly said yes and the professor suggested she come over at lunchtime, telling her he would have lunch for her. Simone thanked him again for the opportunity.

"There's no need to thank me, Simone. Like I said before, you are helping me out. By the way, you can call me Henri here; we don't have to be so formal."

Simone visited Henri's loft several times over the coming weeks as there was still a great deal of work to be done on the project. The upscale loft was palatial compared to her dormitory space; the sleek industrial building was converted from a large automotive factory. Henri's kitchen, living room, and studio area were a massive open-concept loft with a twenty-foot ceiling and ten-foot-tall windows. Simone felt it was the perfect space—there was so much natural light entering from the oversized windows, and no other tall buildings were nearby to block the view of downtown Syracuse.

One evening Simone stayed particularly late, not noticing it was fully dark outside. Henri showed her his spare bedroom, and asked if she would like to use it since he didn't feel it was safe for her to travel home so late. The professor pointed out that his master suite on the other side of the loft had its own bathroom so she would have the hallway bathroom to herself. Simone agreed to use the room that night, and eventually it became a routine for her to stay over on Saturday nights as she didn't feel safe walking back alone in the dark.

The professor was gracious, frequently offering things to make her feel more comfortable, and he cooked great meals every night she stayed over. Then, early Sunday mornings, Simone would walk back to the dorm, something that didn't go unnoticed by her dorm mates.

Norma asked, "Simone, where are you spending your Saturday nights?"

Simone lied, "I stay with my friend who has an apartment off campus. She's always inviting me to come over."

In truth, Simone spent every Saturday at Henri's. After working on their project, they would have conversation and eat dinner together. Simone adored Henri; he was caring and polite, and as time went on, adoration became affection, though she kept her feelings to herself until one evening when Henri confessed his feelings for her. That confession led to a kiss. Simone was elated; she couldn't believe Henri felt the way she did, though her excitement was quelled when he told her they couldn't let anyone know because the university administration didn't approve of professor-student relationships.

****

With Spring Break approaching in a few weeks, Simone had prepared to go back to Brooklyn for the week school was closed, but Henri begged her to spend the week with him in the Florida Keys instead. He showed her a picture of the two-bedroom cottage he had already rented for just the two of them. This was a big step for Simone; she had never gone away with someone before, but she agreed easily—after all, she was in love.

Lying to her mother was extremely difficult. Simone made up a story, telling Laura that she was going away with some girlfriends to Florida. Mrs. Mills was happy that Simone was making new friends; she believed her introverted daughter needed to have more fun. Still prone to worrying about her daughter though, Laura made Simone promise to call her when she arrived in Florida and when returned home safely.

The couple arrived to find that the pastel pink cottage was beautiful and secluded. "Henri, it's so pretty—and look, it's close to the beach," Simone said as they entered the rental unit.

Henri placed her luggage in the smaller bedroom and took his luggage to the other.

"I have to go shopping for a bathing suit," stated Simone.

"I have to buy one too. There weren't any available in Syracuse," said Henri. When Simone exited her room, Henri pulled her into his arms and said, "Why don't we freshen up and then I'll take you shopping. Then we'll go out tonight."

"That sounds exciting, where are we going?" asked Simone.

"It's a surprise," Henri said before kissing her.

The couple went to a local mall, where Henri purchased swim trunks for himself. Simone picked out a simple one-piece bathing suit, but Henri put it back on the rack and selected an expensive sexy bikini instead. He also picked out a fitted, shimmery turquoise mini dress with spaghetti straps, telling her it went well with her beautiful green eyes and auburn hair.

They had dinner at a seaside restaurant on the pier where they watched the sun set on the horizon. Then the couple returned to the cottage to change before going out again, at which point Henri instructed Simone to wear the new dress. She wasn't used to wearing snug dresses and felt a little awkward in it.

"That dress fits you so well, you look gorgeous." The compliment made Simone blush and smile. Henri wore a dark teal suit with a white designer tee. At six foot five and 250 pounds, he was much taller and broader than the 101-pound Simone, who stood at five foot three.

A taxi dropped them off at an upscale nightclub, but when they got out, Simone stopped and turned around.

"Henri, you know I'm only eighteen, I can't go in there." To her surprise, the professor quickly produced a fake ID he'd made from one of the photos he'd taken of her at his loft.

"Wow, you think of everything," she commented. Simone had a wonderful time as they danced all night; and though the rum punch disturbed her balance, she was so grateful that Henri had brought her on the trip. When they returned to the cottage, Simone wanted to walk on the beach in the humid night air, so they took off their shoes and strolled along the shoreline for a few minutes before Henri decided it was time to return.

Once inside, Simone turned to Henri and thanked him again for the wonderful evening. Henri pulled Simone into his arms and kissed her before she could even finish her sentence. He confessed his love for her again, before removing her dress, and that night Simone gave her virginity to Henri. The small bedroom she'd originally been staying in remained empty for the rest of the week.

After the break, the couple returned to Henri's loft with matching tans and secrets. The professor gave Simone a copy of his keys so she could come to the loft at any time. "This is your home away from the dorm," he told her.

While sleeping at Henri's that first night back, Simone was startled by her cell phone in the middle of the night. After viewing the number, she quickly shoved the naked Henri off of her before hitting the talk button.

"Hi Mom, you're calling kind of late," she whispered.

"Simone, you never let me know you'd arrived back to the university safely. I was calling to make sure you were okay."

"Sorry Mom, I forgot. We were so tired when we got back; it wasn't a direct flight."

"That's OK Simi, I figured you forgot; I'll let you get back to sleep. I'm glad you had a good time with your girlfriends. Goodnight." Guilt-ridden, Simone thought seriously about telling her mother the truth until the sleepy professor reached over and pulled Simone close, both quickly drifting off to sleep.

****

Their intimacy brought the student and professor closer; every Saturday and Sunday were spent together; however, little work was being done on the project. Henri suggested Simone add some weekdays to the time they spend together at the loft, but Simone refused. She told him she was afraid her grades would suffer if they spent too much time together, and she was tired of sneaking around like a criminal anyway. Simone wanted a full relationship where they could do things together outside of the loft; more importantly, Simone wanted to tell her mother about Henri so that she could stop lying to her. Henri was vehemently against her suggestions. This led to the couple's first fight; and Simone packed her things to leave. The professor tried to reason with his lover, but Simone had already run out the door, refusing to come back to the loft. Henri stopped short of following her into the hallway; he didn't want to make a scene where his neighbors could hear them.

Simone stayed away from Henri for the rest of the week, ignoring his constant texts and voicemails, all begging her to speak to him. Of course, she was forced to face him in class, and he looked so sad when she took her quiz paper out of his hand. That night, she returned to the loft. Henri apologized for arguing and convinced her to stay the night. He promised to take her somewhere special the following weekend to make up for it.

Henri's weekend excursion was to a couples-only resort in the Poconos. The romantic suite, designed with pink shag carpeting and a heart-shaped tub, wasn't Simone's taste, but she tolerated it because Henri loved the room. That evening, after they made love, Henri gave her a gold heart bracelet with their names inscribed together. In Simone's mind, it was a sign that their relationship had reached a higher level. The eighteen-year-old freshman was in love with her 34-year-old Dutch professor, and she imagined a marriage proposal would follow soon so they wouldn't have to hide their relationship anymore. Her parents still knew nothing of the romance, they only knew that she'd stopped complaining about how boring things were at school.

Then, just as the semester was coming to an end in May, Simone was once again summoned out of class to sit before the dean.

"Good morning, Ms. Mills," he said. Then, getting straight to the point, "It was brought to my attention that you and Professor Janssen are in an intimate relationship. You may not be aware of this, but faculty members are not allowed to have intimate relations with their current students. I've just had a meeting with Professor Janssen, and as of today, he has been removed from his position at this school. The art department chairman will be taking over all of Mr. Janssen's classes. He will also review any high grades you received from Professor Janssen, so you may receive a call to meet with him shortly."

Simone started crying. "We haven't done anything wrong."

"Ms. Mills, I don't mean to upset you, but this is for the best. I'm sure you weren't aware that Mr. Janssen is a married man with children."

Simone was stunned. "No...no, this can't be true, Henri's not married."

"Yes, unfortunately it is true Ms. Mills. He returns occasionally to the Netherlands to see them."

Distraught, Simone cried all the way back to her room, receiving strange looks from many people as she walked through the hallway. When she arrived back to her dorm, she saw Lisa sitting in the room with a big smile. Simone immediately knew who the snitch was. Later, Norma confirmed that Lisa had told everyone about her affair after finding Simone's phone in the common area. Simone knew she had never left her phone in the common area, and suspected Lisa had been going through her personal space again.

Not caring to deal with her dorm mate in the moment, Simone ran out of the room with her cell phone and called Henri; but the phone rang until it went to voicemail. "Henri, is it true, are you really married? Please Henri, tell me the truth," was the message she left. With her backpack slung over one shoulder, Simone's swift walk turned into a sprint as she headed for the loft. She let herself into the building with the key she was given, thankful the place was quiet as she entered the elevator. At first she knocked repeatedly on the door; but it never opened. Then Simone tried opening it with the key Henri had given her, but the deadbolt prevented her from entering. Simone knew the bolt could only be locked from the inside.

She ran back to her room to do her own investigation on her laptop. It didn't take long before Simone was looking at pictures of Henri with his wife in Holland—the dean hadn't been lying. And all information indicated that they were still married. She stayed in bed for the rest of the day crying, not caring about her missed classes. The heartbreak and anger she felt were overwhelming. For days, Simone attended classes with puffy eyes. The realization that Henri had taken advantage of her and her inexperience made her feel like a fool. She tossed his keys and all his gifts into the trash.

Things did not get better when Matt, Lisa's boyfriend, blocked her path in the hallway one day. He told her that he didn't agree with what Lisa had done, then he asked if she would go out with him. Simone said nothing, just pushed him out of her way and kept walking. Matt became angry, yelling, "Oh, you think you're too good for me? No, I forgot, you only do professors!"

Simone was grateful when the semester came to an end.

Back at home, she hid her heartbreak from her family; all memories of Henri and her broken heart buried, covered by a thick scab of anger, and shoved to the back of her mind. When school reopened that fall, Simone devoted all her time and energy to her studies. She ignored party invitations and kept to herself. Her only goal was to complete college and leave it behind as fast as possible.

When she reached the end of her junior year, her college advisor knew she wanted to pursue a graduate degree, so, together they looked over her grades and sorted out the scholarships and other financial grants she should apply for.

"Simone, your grades are fantastic, but many scholarships require students to have extracurricular activities. You haven't joined any clubs or sports since you came here. You must join a club before graduating," he said. Simone sighed as she thought of all the club activities she had been invited to that she had immediately turned down. The advisor gave her a long list of activities to choose from, but she didn't know where to start. Many were sports teams, which required extra hours for travelling or practice, and Simone didn't want to spend more time than was necessary to be a member, so she crossed all those out. After reviewing the remaining list of clubs, Simone decided to join the Christian club, figuring it would be easy and not take up too much time.

After that, Simone attended the semi-weekly Christian club meetings; usually sitting in the back, hoping no one noticed her in the crowd. She observed the members who, during greetings, really seemed to care for one another. She noticed that they made a point to support individuals who were going through tough ordeals. Some meetings turned into group therapy sessions where the person who was in some type of distress was prayed over. Occasionally, an attendee would stand up and give a testimony of what they'd achieved or what they were currently going through, and all meetings ended with a group prayer. Simone held hands with strangers, pretending to pray, but it was all very confusing to her. The services she'd attended at her family's church wasn't like this, they never held hands with strangers or attended service in jeans.

Simone had seen Leslie, one of the regular attendees, around campus; she'd always seemed so upbeat and cheerful. One day, Leslie testified about her struggle with depression since grade school. She'd been prescribed a variety of psychiatric medications, and many had helped, but Leslie also felt becoming a member of a faith-based community provided mental health benefits. She explained how she'd joined the Christian club and attended regular service in an outside church—solely for health benefits—and it had worked. Leslie's doctor decreased her meds, and today she felt and expressed her emotions better; but she'd found so much more than a membership. Leslie had found that having a relationship with Christ had given her a peace she had never experienced before.

Intrigued by the testimony she'd heard, Simone struck up the nerve to question Leslie about her experiences. They started meeting in the cafeteria for conversations and soon Simone considered Leslie to be her first real college friend. For the first time, Simone told another person all that had happened between herself and the professor. She needed to know how Leslie would have handled it all.

"Well," Leslie told her, "resisting premarital sex is a huge issue for most people. Christians are told to resist because God wants only married couples to have sex. This doesn't make sense to the secular world; they believe God forbids sex other than between married couples because He doesn't want anyone to enjoy life, but the truth is the opposite. He wants the best for us. God wants people to enjoy life and the best way to do that is to fully commit only to your spouse. Genesis 2:24 says that a man is to leave his father and mother and unite with his wife, the two becoming one flesh. Marriage is not just for sex; it's a commitment to stay together, to take care of one another. It's also the optimal environment God wants children to be born into. However, if a Christian makes a mistake and commits any sin, the sin is to be confessed and genuinely repented. As a member of the body of Christ, we know that Jesus forgives our sins and carries our burdens. I'm not saying nothing bad happens to people after they give their life to Him; Christ never promised that nothing bad will happen after you accept Him, but if something bad does happen, I know I can ask for, and expect, help.

"So, as a Christian, I would confess and repent of the sin I committed. It can be tough on relationships because most guys want sex with no commitment, but I pray that the right guy will respect my faith and ask for marriage before sex."

Listening to Leslie's answer made Simone see clearly that, had she been a Christian when she met Henri, he wouldn't have been able to use her.

Simone wanted the connection and peace that Leslie had. She asked Leslie to pray for her, and the woman did. Leslie also helped Simone pray for herself.

Before the end of her senior year, Simone had given her life to Christ. There were no flashing lights and she didn't hear a voice in her head, but the peace she felt when she made the commitment was real.

Simone called her family and gave them the great news. Their response to her accepting Christ into her life was lackluster; they were content that she was happy about her experience, but it didn't mean anything to them. Although Simone's parents considered themselves to be Christians, her mother was the only one who attended church services, and her attendance was only during major holidays like Christmas and Easter; her father had rarely come along on any church trip, and Simone didn't think he'd been to any since the divorce. And while there was always a Bible in their library when Simone was growing up, no one read it; the book was left undisturbed, stacked against the dictionary and other reference books.

Martin had no interest in her newfound relationship with Christ; his concern was for her plans after graduation. When Simone gave Martin a list of graduate schools she planned to apply to, one that included a long shot, the prestigious Royal College of Art in London, her brother instructed her to not waste her time on that one.

Leslie bought a Bible for Simone and invited her to attend her church. It was in church that Simone learned, after hearing many testimonies from other worshipers, that being a Christian does not equal being a perfect person. Some church members had sordid or unsavory pasts; others were trapped in their own versions of hell. But when you looked at their faces or studied their character, you would never know of the trauma or tragedy that they went, or were going through. These were loving, forgiving individuals who continually reached out to help others. It didn't take long for Simone to join Leslie's church, eventually even becoming a member of the choir.

The Sunday before she completed her senior-year coursework, Simone reluctantly said goodbye to all her new Christian club and church member friends. For her last service, the choir director arranged for Simone to have a long solo as a farewell present. Simone chose a relatively new Christian worship song that she'd fallen in love with, and when the solo came to an end, many stood and applauded. Some people even had tears in their eyes because they were so moved. Before she left, the pastor and congregants all gave her hugs, and all prayed for her success.

****

It was late May when the graduate returned to her Brooklyn home. Laura was so happy to have her daughter living with her again, she arranged more than a few outings for just the two of them. Simone's lodging at her graduate school, The Royal School of Art in London, wouldn't be available for several weeks, so Laura wanted to make the most of the time they would have together.

Over the years, the lies Simone had told her mother during freshman year weighed on her mind; occasionally she would pick up her phone with the intention of telling her mother everything that had happened, but her indecisiveness never allowed her to go through with the plan. There were times when she'd made up her mind that it was a secret never to be revealed; however, spending the extra time together made Simone realize how much she'd missed coming to her mom with whatever problem she had.

So, after gathering her nerve, Simone sat with her mother one morning before she left for London. She revealed everything that had taken place with Henri before relaying the lie about the Spring Break trip. Simone then shared what had happened in the aftermath and described what her life was like after the affair ended. She also apologized to her mother for lying.

Laura was furious, and Simone was completely unprepared for mother's reaction. Fuming, Laura accused Simone of allowing herself to become a married man's whore, and she compared her daughter to Cindy. The statement stung like a slap in the face, and it churned up all those negative feelings she'd felt in her freshman year.

Mother and daughter didn't speak to one another for the rest of the day. That evening, Simone received a call from her father. It didn't take long to learn that her mother had called him to share her story. He didn't call her names like Laura had, but he did express how disappointed he was in Simone's behavior. She wanted to say the same to him, but Simone kept her mouth shut so the conversation would end quicker; she didn't want to argue with her parents anymore. On that day she vowed never to reveal her problems to her parents again. *There's just some information they don't need to know*, she reasoned.

****

For the rest of her time at her mom's, Simone stayed out of the house as much as possible to avoid the awkward, oppressive silence emanating from her mother. They were cordial to each other when they did speak, but the tension was stifling to Simone. This was a new experience for her personally, though she'd seen the scenario before. She remembered observing Laura's tight-lipped silent treatment with her father after they argued. The treatment made her best friend's house a respite from home. Marcy and Simone became best friends in their middle school drama class; gossiping about their parents and telling secrets was always on their agenda, but Marcy was completely shocked when Simone finally told her the story of Henri.

"Simone, that's the last thing I expected to hear from you. I mean, you were such a nerd in high school; a pretty nerd who never went on a date, even with all the cute guys asking you out. You went from not dating at all to having an affair with your professor as a freshman? All I can say is, wow. You've blown my mind. Your mother was understandably shocked, but the comments she made were mean and hurtful. Wait, didn't she put you on the pill when you were in high school? She must have expected you to have sex at some point?"

"Yes, but at the time she said it was just a precaution, and that she didn't expect me to put it to use. Maybe my parents would have been happier if I started having sex in high school. I'm twenty-two-years old, yet they're chastising me like a child. I can't believe my dad, of all people, was shaming me. I messed up, I know that, even though I had no idea that Henri was married. Anyway, it'll never happen again. From now on, I'll stay celibate until I get married."

"Oh come on; you're moving to London. British accents are very sexy. Some irresistible Londoner will make you forget all about your vow, and when you call for advice, I'll say, 'I told you so.'"

"No Marcy, I told you before that my life has changed; I'm serious about my faith. I vowed to remain celibate because God says not to have sex outside of marriage. Also, it saves me from being duped by men."

"Well, OK then," said Marcy as she nodded her head. She'd never seen her friend so certain about anything before. "I admire your fortitude, and I know you will accomplish anything you set your mind to, but be careful that you don't chase away the one man who was meant for you."

"Well, if I meet 'the one,' he'd have to respect my wishes for us to be together. But at this point in my life, I'm not going to stress about finding someone."

****

The next morning, Simone confirmed with her new school that she could move into the housing unit earlier than planned—leaving home ASAP to escape her stern mother was all she could think of. But she kept her new departure date to herself until the evening before her flight, and Laura was startled when Simone informed her of the early departure.

"Simone I don't understand, why are you leaving three weeks early?" she asked as she searched Simone's face for an answer.

I don't understand you, Mom, didn't you want me to leave? was what she thought, but didn't have the heart to say, when her mother looked so disheartened. "I, ahh, thought an early move would give me time to get acquainted with London. Don't worry about reaching me—remember, we can video chat whenever you want to see me."

Still stunned, Laura didn't know what to say as Simone rolled her bags out the front door the next morning. Simone turned and gave Laura a hug before handing her luggage to the Uber driver. "I'll text you when I land," said Simone.

The Boeing 777 aircraft touched down at Heathrow Airport in the early evening. Heathrow's massive terminal, a city unto itself, overwhelmed the young graduate student. Other passengers from her flight stood by the luggage carousel, but Simone sat down to take in her surroundings. A quick call to her mother took the sting out of the loneliness she'd felt on her first solo flight out of the country.

The cultural differences took some getting used to; however, unlike her experience with her undergrad roommates, Simone got along extremely well with her grad school flat mate, Nikki, and the two became close friends.

CHAPTER FIVE
SESSIONS

Simone awoke early Sunday morning and prepared two outfits: a black skirt and a baby blue cashmere sweater for church, and her new dress for her lunch meeting. She hopped in her car and took off for church alone as usual; Nikki and Derrick had always declined her invites to attend Sunday morning services. That wasn't surprising: most of her British friends and associates never attended church, save for weddings and funerals. Simone thought it strange that the country that produced the most popular translation of the Bible, the King James version, has very few church attenders. Simone wouldn't describe herself as deeply religious, but she'd given her life to Christ with the intention to live like a true follower regardless of where she lived, so regular church attendance was necessary.

Back when she'd informed her pastor in Syracuse that she was moving to London, he'd directed her towards a West London Church pastored by a friend of his. Unlike Pastor Lawrence's small Syracuse church, the Family Assemblies of God Church in Guildford was a massive megachurch congregation of more than 2,000 members. Many of the regular members attended both Sunday and midweek services. The drive was over an hour from her home in Acton, but it was worth it; the members were as unpretentious and welcoming as those at Pastor Lawrence's church.

Rebecca Standish was one of the first church members Simone met when she arrived. Despite her position on the church board, there was something about Becky's character that made Simone feel at ease and less homesick for her former church. Since then, they'd worked together on various projects, including upgrading the church's website and designing the set for the children's Christmas play. The thirty-six-year-old social worker had become a church member as a teenager, and she was well respected by the members, and was someone whom Simone, as a new Christian, looked to for help with scripture interpretation.

Today, Simone left the church later than planned because she needed to find Becky and discuss the details of their next small group meeting before she could leave. That done, Simone arrived home with only twenty minutes left to get ready. She took a quick shower and applied a little makeup before dressing. The dress she'd purchased with Nikki clung to her body more than she remembered, and suspicious, Simone checked the tag and realized with dread that Nikki had switched the dress to the smaller size. "I can't believe she did that!" she screamed. But there was no time to find something else to wear, so Simone picked up her phone and quickly texted Nikki, "*I know what you did and I will deal with you upon my return!*" followed with a string of mean emojis.

She heard her business phone ringing, and was about to let the answering machine take it but then realized it could be Thomas. Simone ran to pick up the phone, almost out of breath when she got to it. "Hello?"

"*Wow, that's a very sexy hello, Simone; I wanted to make sure you weren't standing me up, it's almost 2:20,"* Thomas said casually.

"Oh no, I'm so sorry, I didn't realize it was so late!"

"Don't worry, you take as much time as you need; the driver will wait. He's parked outside your shop in a grey sedan with tinted windows."

"I'm almost ready, I just have to grab a few things and I'm out the door." Simone put on her leather jacket and grabbed her purse before rushing out.

As promised, there was a sedan double-parked outside her shop. The driver, dressed in a black cap and shades, opened the back door and closed it behind her after she was seated. Simone had had the strange feeling that someone was looking at her backside when she entered the back seat; and when she looked up to see who was around, she caught Derrick peering through his window at the sedan with a stern look. *"What was that about?"* she wondered. The car drove off immediately, and since the driver didn't seem interested in conversation, Simone settled in and took out her phone. Nikki had texted her back: *"YOU'RE WELCOME!"*

Simone saw many restaurants when they drove through the streets of Richmond, but the car continued its journey through Richmond Park; she wondered what restaurant could be in this area. Richmond Park was known to have many spacious homes for the rich, but no commercial district. A few seconds later, the car slowed and turned into a dark, narrow driveway, though Simone was certain there was no restaurant nearby. When the driver used his smartphone to open the gate, they passed through, and Simone gasped when she saw that the driveway led to a stunning white stone mansion. Tall poplar trees lined the perimeter of the property, creating an excellent privacy screen.

Simone surmised that this had to be Thomas Lloyd's home.

The driver opened the door and took her hand to assist her out of the vehicle, then immediately removed the cap and dark shades. It was Thomas! All Simone could do was gasp. Clearly enjoying his deception, Thomas laughed heartily at her expression.

"You chauffeured for me and Alistair, so I figured it was the least I could do for you," he said. She couldn't help but laugh with him.

"You tricked me! I thought you were taking me out for lunch."

"Oh no, I did not trick you; I am taking you to have lunch, only at my home. I hope that's alright with you. After Thursday's paparazzi attack, I decided to lay low for a few days. Lunch should be ready though, so let me escort you inside," he said as he extended his arm. Simone took it and allowed him to lead the way. When they entered the spacious foyer, an elderly grey-haired woman approached them.

"Good afternoon, Mr. Lloyd; lunch will be served in five minutes. Would you like me to take your jackets?" she asked.

"Thanks Libby, that would be great. I'd like to introduce you to a new friend of mine; this is Ms. Simone Mills."

"It's a pleasure to meet you, Ms. Mills," said Libby with a smile.

"Thank you, it's nice to meet you, too," said Simone.

"We'll be back when you're ready, Libby. I'll show Ms. Mills around in the meantime." Thomas then looked at Simone and asked, "Would you like to see the gardens?"

"Yes, that would be nice," she said.

Thomas led Simone through a few rooms to the rear of the home. She was very impressed with the interior design; the décor was posh and comfortable at the same time. Somehow the mix of contemporary and traditional pieces went together seamlessly. They exited through a sunroom onto a raised deck.

A garden path took them through a wall of hedges that led to an herb garden. Simone was greeted by the intoxicating fragrances of lavender and mint; she identified batches of fuchsia, primrose, and a variety of other low-height flowering perennials. The path continued through rows of rose shrubs. Beyond the flowering shrubs were huge raised planter beds filled with vegetables. Simone admired tall purple-stemmed kale, savory cabbages, heirloom tomatoes, and eggplant, along with other items.

"I love your garden, especially the lavender and those massive rosemary shrubs. I've tried so hard to grow rosemary in my small garden, but the plants never thrive. The roots always rot," she said.

"Maybe you're overwatering them; try to let the ground dry out between watering," suggested Thomas.

"Hmmm, you sound very much like a gardener," Simone said, turning to him.

"Well, that's because I *am* the gardener," he said.

Simone laughed. "Thomas Lloyd, the famous rocker, is a gardener? You're trying to trick me again."

"No it's true; of course I hired a professional to design the landscape, and someone maintains the garden when I'm away; but whenever I'm home, I'm the gardener."

"Really? How long have you had this hobby, and when did you start it?" she asked.

"Well let's see; how much do you know about my background and lifestyle?" Thomas asked sheepishly.

"I'm familiar with some of your earlier music, but I haven't been able to keep up with anything outside my field for the past few years. All my time has been devoted to completing my studies and obtaining my work permit."

"Why don't we sit over here," Thomas suggested, motioning to a stone bench at the center of the garden. From their position, Simone could see the back of the Richmond Park woods. No homes or fences obstructed the picturesque view of the open woods and its wildflowers. "The only way I know how to honestly answer your question is to start from the beginning," he began.

"There was a time when my face was plastered on the cover of some rag every week, sometimes several times a week. Reason being, I had a very bad drug habit. I'm deeply embarrassed of some of the things I've done. The media covered every aspect of it.

"My habit began with me popping pills to relieve anxiety before going onstage. After a while, the pills weren't helping anymore, so I graduated to cocaine, and sometimes opioids. You'd be surprised at how many people in the industry were hooked; the women I dated, backstage staff; every award show had drugs somewhere. Anyway, the people I hung out with, the ones I thought were friends, encouraged me to keep using because they were hooked themselves, and I always picked up the tab. It didn't take long for my habit to become a full-blown addiction. Eventually, my performances suffered, then my health went downhill. I'd show up late for rehearsals, and just forget a lot of important stuff. My grandmother and brother tried to make me stop, but instead of taking their advice, I pushed them away.

"Gran is very special to me; she raised me and my brother because, after my father died in a car accident, my mother had to work long hours in the shop my parents had purchased. Gran stayed with us every day. It was my gran who, when my music teacher told her that I was gifted, made sure I had proper piano lessons; I owe my success to her. She fed us, and made sure we did our homework. She even took us to church.

"Anyway, one day she visited me and I was stoned out of my mind. I remember trying to stand up to give her a hug, but I was too high. She argued with me as usual, but it was the look on her face that did me in. That look showed me how disappointed she was in what I'd become. I felt so ashamed that she was seeing me like that.

"Gran stayed with me that day. She kicked out my so-called friends and helped me get into a good rehab program. Part of my recovery was determining why I started using in the first place, and my counselor made me realize I was using drugs to self-medicate for anxiety and stress. He suggested I try different hobbies to develop healthier habits. I like playing football, but it's not something I can do every day. There were other trial hobbies, but believe it or not, gardening was the one thing I really enjoyed that I could maintain. Guess there's a little farmer in me somewhere.

"So, the longwinded answer to your question is, I started gardening after rehab. I enjoy it because gardening de-stresses me," said Thomas.

"Well, I for one am very happy you found something positive to do that helped with your illness," she said. Thomas was amazed that Simone was so nonchalant about his former drug addiction. He was even more surprised with himself for divulging so much about his personal life, as he'd had no intention of going into so much depth. But it seemed, just as when he'd been in her car, he found Simone quite easy to talk to.

They walked back inside to the dining room, where Libby had laid out a sumptuous spread of dishes. There was cottage pie, grilled sea bass with new potatoes, cabbage, and onions, along with freshly baked brown bread. Thomas pulled out Simone's chair and said, "See, I'm not the wild rock star you see on stage; I'm a gentleman."

Simone laughed, "Unfortunately I've never had the opportunity to see you on stage! Your tickets were always sold out."

"Well, I promise you free tickets the next time we perform in London," he said.

"I'd love that; it would be wonderful," said Simone.

Thomas picked up and opened a bottle of chilled wine that had been left in a basket. "I hope you like this Pinot Noir. It's a favorite of mine, but I have others if you don't care for it," he said as he poured. Simone swirled the wine in her glass and sniffed, discovering that there was a faint fruit fragrance to it. She sipped a little and allowed the liquid to rest in her mouth before swallowing. The bouquet of fruit flavors was almost overwhelming, and Simone moaned a little and briefly closed her eyes.

"This is the best wine I've had in a very long time." Simone turned over the bottle to read the label. "Willamette Valley, Oregon. Oregon! I had no idea there were vineyards in Oregon."

"Oregon is not well known by some for wine, but that's to my advantage. I've invested in this particular vineyard because I had the same reaction to the wine that you just did," said Thomas. Simone was slightly embarrassed when she remembered that she'd actually moaned.

They conversed throughout the meal. She found Thomas very easy to talk to, not at all what she'd expected from a celebrity. He was open and honest about every aspect of his life, and there was no hint of pretension.

They were discussing Simone's love of portrait painting when her host surprised her: "Would you mind painting me? The band doesn't tour for another two months; would that be enough time?" he asked.

"Mind?! I'd love to paint you, and that's plenty of time. When would you be available?" Simone asked eagerly. They made arrangements for Thomas to come to Simone's shop on Wednesday and Friday afternoons starting that week.

After that, Thomas continued to ask about Simone's career. Then they discussed their families. He talked about his brother, James, his niece and nephews. Simone told Thomas of her parents' divorce and how it had affected the dynamics of her whole family. When she told him she'd found Christ in college of all places, Thomas was intrigued.

"I don't understand, how does one 'find' Christ? Do you just start saying you believe in Him?" he asked.

"No, it's more than that and so much more important. Finding Christ means you give your life to Him. You accept Him as your Lord and Savior and you believe that He died on the cross for your sins. You also let Him live through you. When you observe someone who is a Christ-follower, you should see the characteristics of Christ in them. Their actions, the way they live their life, the comments they make; it should all reveal Christ's character in them. Anyone can say they believe in Him; the devil also believes that Christ exists, but that doesn't make him a follower of Christ. A follower has to study His words, pray and believe He is their Savior to develop a relationship with Him," said Simone.

"That's interesting, I've never heard it explained quite that way before," said Thomas as

Libby came through the door with a black forest cake.

"Oh Libby, that looks delicious, but I don't know if I should have any; it looks so rich and chocolaty," said Simone.

"Please tell me you're not going to let me eat dessert alone," said Thomas.

"Well, I'll just have a small piece," said Simone. Libby served them both a slice. "This is truly delicious," said Simone as she ate.

"Would you like some coffee with it?" asked Thomas.

"No, but thank you." Simone glanced at the window and noticed how dark the sky had become. Then she looked at the clock. "Oh my gosh, it's 8:30. You've been so gracious, and I've been taking up all of your Sunday evening," said Simone.

"You haven't taken up my time. We've been having a wonderful conversation, and I had no other plans for today," said Thomas.

Simone stood from her chair. "Thank you Thomas, it was so sweet of you to invite me into your home. I had a great time and the meal was wonderful; thank you so much for this."

"Just wait here a minute and I will grab our jackets and my chauffeur hat," he said.

"Oh no, you don't have to drive me back, I'll take a taxi," said Simone.

"No taxi is needed, the chauffeur will take you back as planned," he said with a smile. A couple moments later, Thomas returned with their jackets and helped Simone into hers before putting his own on. Then he extended his arm for her to hold onto as they exited his home.

The evening's chilled wind seem to blow right through her thin jacket, and Thomas felt her shiver, so he stopped and took off his jacket and draped it around her shoulders before they continued.

"Thank you Thomas, you're such a gentleman."

"See, I told you so," he said and they both laughed. They continued conversing when they got in the car, and the trip home seemed so much shorter to Simone. Thomas double-parked again in front of her shop, then got out and opened the back door, still playing the chauffeur role. But as he helped her out of the car, he bent down and kissed her hand.

Simone was awestruck. She said jokingly, "Thank you, Mr. Chauffeur. With service like this you'll always be on call." They both laughed and said their goodbyes before Thomas stepped back into the vehicle.

****

When Derrick heard the car drive up, he immediately went to his window and was surprised as he watched the driver kiss Simone's hand. Then he heard laughter and wondered why she was so friendly with a chauffeur. He decided to question Simone during their next coffee meeting.

****

Simone found herself humming one of Thomas's songs as she walked into her home. She called Nikki as soon as she was settled and filled her in on every detail of the lunch.

"Now aren't you glad I switched the dress size?" said Nikki.

"Nikki you are terrible. I had no intention of accentuating my rear end. Thankfully Thomas was a gentleman and didn't notice that my dress was too tight."

"How do you feel after going on a date with Thomas Lloyd?" asked Nikki.

"It was not a date, it was a thank-you lunch," said Simone.

"I have news for you miss, thank-you lunches don't take six hours. I'd be gob smacked if he didn't ask you over again, or maybe he'll give you a ring later in the week," said Nikki.

"Well," Simone started, "he will be here when I begin painting his portrait."

"Wait, what's this, are you holding out on me? You've already set up the next date? That's wonderful!" Nikki gushed.

"It's not a date, it's a portrait appointment that I have to finish within two months."

"Hmmm, I don't know what they call it in the States, but in England, it's called a date. You'd better not let Derrick know."

"What do you mean? Why would Derrick care?" said Simone.

"I believe he has a thing for you; Derrick brings you up in most of our conversations. He's been having coffee and conversation with you every week since forever."

"Well, I don't know about in England, but in the States, two people can drink coffee at work in the morning and not have a thing for each other."

"I hope you're right, but sometimes when I see the way he looks at you, I get the feeling that it's more than a friendly look. Could be he's afraid to approach you for fear of rejection."

"Nikki, Derrick's known me for almost a year. If he had a thing for me, he would've said something by now." The two continued chatting on the phone until they said their goodnights.

****

Thomas was on Simone's mind every day. Besides being excited for the opportunity to paint a celebrity, she was looking forward to getting the time to have conversations with her new friend.

Ensuring that she was well prepared, Simone purchased an expensive linen canvas and new brushes for the occasion, and when the day of the appointment came, she placed a prepared platter of sandwiches and sliced fruit on a small table close to where Thomas would sit. Simone dressed in a pair of dark skinny jeans and a fashion tee, her typical paint gear. She was certain Nikki would frown on her selection, but painting calls for practicality since paint had a way of getting on your clothes no matter how careful you were. At 5 PM she immediately flipped her door sign to "We are now closed."

Looking out the glass door of her shop, Simone watched as Thomas's gunmetal-grey Porsche slowed in front of her establishment and parked a few doors down. As Thomas exited his vehicle in a velvet navy blazer, expensive-looking denim pants, and shades, Simone unconsciously studied his profile, noting that he was about six feet tall and lean but not skinny. He looked up and caught her observing him through the door and responded with a grin that she was becoming familiar with. Simone stepped out the door to welcome him in, and Thomas gave her a brief hello hug before entering. Inside the shop, he studied the framed photography work displayed on the wall intently.

"Are all of these your work?" he asked.

"Yes," she replied.

"You are very talented. How long have you been open for business?" he asked.

"Thank you, I'm glad you like my work. This December will mark my first year in business," she said as she began closing the window blinds. "I'm doing this to control the lighting, it has to be the same for every sitting. Please help yourself to the platter. I also have a pot of coffee on," she said.

"No thank you, I'm not hungry now, maybe I'll have something later."

"Well then, let's get started. I want you to relax for a few minutes before I move you into a pose; it has to be a comfortable position since you'll have to hold it for a while. Why don't you come over here and let me position you in this armchair," said Simone as she led him by the arm. She loved the scent of his cologne, but decided not to tell Thomas; she didn't want him to get the wrong impression. Simone continued to instruct Thomas, then moved his hand and lifted his chin slightly to the side. When she was done, Simone walked to the wall and turned up the lighting. "For this initial sitting, I'm focusing on your shape and background, so don't worry too much about keeping perfectly still."

"Great, maybe we can continue our conversation from Sunday."

"That's fine with me," said Simone.

"After you left, I began remembering things my grandmother used to tell me. You know she used to take me to church in spite of my mother's beliefs," he said.

"What does your mother believe?" said Simone.

"Mother doesn't believe there's anything other than this life."

"And what do you believe?"

"I guess you can say I'm agnostic because I'm not sure if God exists. I see both evidence to the contrary and evidence that suggests there has to be a higher power. I don't believe my ancestors came from a rock, but I also don't believe we are all controlled by a master puppeteer who occasionally creates disease and earthquakes just to stir things up," said Thomas.

"Well, I'm not an expert in apologetics but you're correct on both beliefs. There is no scientific proof to the theory that we are descendants from bacteria or minerals found in rocks. Also, there's no explanation for who or what created the special bacteria and minerals in the first place. As for the other theory, there's no place in the Bible that says Christ came to bring us suffering and pain. It's actually the opposite. In Jeremiah 29:11, he says that the Lord told him, 'For I know the plans I have in mind for you. They are plans for peace not disaster.' And Jesus didn't give His disciples the authority to inflict disease, He gave them the authority to heal every disease and every affliction. Some people say disasters are an act of God, but they are wrong. Because we live on earth, we are subject to the properties and forces on earth; like gravity, friction, and temperature—these things cause natural disasters. God gave us the earth and free will to do as we please. He doesn't control us like a puppeteer; if that were true, murder wouldn't exist, because God is against murder. He doesn't control the man who picks up a weapon to kill another man. God does not obtain joy from our sorrow; He doesn't rejoice when we die at the hand of another, but He receives our spirit after we experience physical death so we never truly die."

"That sort of makes sense," said Thomas.

"What were some of the things your grandmother used to tell you?" asked Simone.

"She continuously encouraged me and my brother to pray, to follow the commandments; you know, things like that. There are so many rules to remember, how does one keep up with them?"

"It's simpler than you think. You don't have to remember all the laws and commandments; just the two most important ones."

"Ah, let me guess: Thou shalt not murder or tell a lie?"

"No, Christ said the two greatest commandments are to love the Lord your God with all your heart, and all your soul, and all your mind, and to love your neighbor as yourself. When you think about the ten commandments, the first four pertain to loving God, the remaining six pertain to loving your neighbor. If everyone kept these two commandments there would be no war, starvation, rape, murder, the list goes on. So, if you're ever confused about how God wants you to live, apply these commandments to every decision you make."

"That's pretty deep. I wish the fanatical paparazzi photographer who posted that picture of your car would follow these commandments," he said.

"Do you know the photographer?" Simone asked.

"Yes, unfortunately he's been following me around for years, ever since we had an altercation."

"What happened?"

"A few years ago, when I was still using, my friends and

I exited a club and this one photographer, Mark Lemmings, shoved his camera right into me. I lost my temper and punched him in the face. It happened very quickly and I did it without thinking. All of his paparazzi buddies took pictures of it, and the photos were on the cover of every paper in England. Of course, he sued me; but the judge found us both at fault so I didn't have to pay him anything; on top of that, he also lost his job. His paper didn't like when their photographers became the headline for other publications. Anyway, Lemmings has had it in for me ever since. This happened more than five years ago, and I'm not a top-ten artist anymore, but he still tries to keep me in the news. Since I've been off drugs, I haven't done anything crazy, so you'd think he'd move onto his next victim; but no, it seems like he insists on stalking me for the rest of my days."

"Have you tried apologizing for your actions; or talking to him, maybe resolving the issue so that he would leave you alone?" asked Simone.

"Are you joking? Why would I apologize for his mistake? Besides, I couldn't get near him without his snapping a hundred photos per second."

"Speaking of photos, I need you to stay still for a minute. I'm going to take a few pictures of your pose before I give you a short break and make some coffee."

"Isn't that cheating?" Thomas said teasingly.

"No, I'm not cheating, I'm just keeping a visual record of your seating position so that when you return, I can place you in the exact same lighting and pose." Simone moved around, taking pictures from different angles. "OK, I'm done. You can get up and move around now."

"Great, mind if I use your loo?" he asked.

"Sure, let me show you where it is." Simone's diminutive apartment contained a cramped bathroom just outside her bedroom, and the bedroom door was wide open, so Thomas could view Simone's small garden through the French doors at the back of the room.

"Do you mind if I took a look at your garden?" he asked.

"No, but it's a little embarrassing. There's not much to look at and I haven't been giving it much attention lately," said Simone. Thomas opened the French doors and stepped out. He walked around the small herb garden and stooped down to study the rotting rosemary plants.

"These aren't completely dead you know. You could save them by improving the drainage. You've planted in a low spot in your garden, so all the rain water pools around the roots of the plant. They must be elevated; but there's no way to do it without digging them up."

"That sounds like a project. I'll have to wait until the weekend to take care of that. We'd better go in now." Thomas put his arm around Simone's waist to assist her back up the steps to her bedroom. Unbeknownst to them, Derrick was looking out his back window, frowning when he witnessed the intimate gesture.

Later, Simone finished the second half of their session and then walked Thomas out to his Porsche.

"Thank you so much for doing this, Thomas. I know you have better things to do with your time, so I wanted to tell you that I'm very grateful that you're giving me so much of it."

"Anything for a friend." Thomas bent down to her petite frame and gave Simone a quick hug and kiss on the cheek. She waved her friend off after he got into the Porsche then Simone touched her cheek as she stood on the curb and watched him drive away. Somehow, the small kiss had given her a wonderful feeling she hadn't experienced in a long time. But then she shook her head and forced herself to stop thinking of it.

As she continued to gaze down the road, Derrick walked up to her. "Simone, what are you looking at?"

"Oh, hi Derrick, that was one of my clients, I'm working on a portrait project for him." She muttered "goodnight" before walking back inside to prevent Derrick from asking more questions. It was important to her that she kept Thomas's identity a secret.

CHAPTER SIX
OSCAR

Derrick entered the studio Friday morning as usual. That morning, Simone had baked fresh banana bread, and Derrick was very appreciative of this dessert and took extra slices to go, though he had no idea that Simone had baked two loaves to make sure to have something for Thomas when he arrived.

For Simone, the rest of Friday dragged on, and it was difficult to stay focused on her work. She played relaxing music and opened her laptop to play with some designs for a custom furniture store. When her phone notified her of the 5 PM appointment, Simone walked to her studio window and watched for the Porsche, but it never arrived. When the wall clock showed 5:20 PM, Simone sighed, thinking that Thomas had found something better to do on a Friday afternoon. She locked the door and peered out the glass door window again. The only new vehicle that drove up was a commercial pickup truck, and Simone watched the grey-haired workman exit the vehicle and make his way to her door. It was only after she opened it that she realized it was Thomas. He gave her a hug and kiss before they stepped inside.

"Wow, you fooled me again; why the elaborate disguise?" she asked.

"Libby spotted Lemmings outside my driveway this morning, so I thought it wise to throw the hound off my scent. I borrowed the gardener's truck and loaned him my Porsche; he had no complaints. And I also keep some disguise materials in the house just in case." Thomas wore overalls, thick glasses, and a grey wig under a dusty workman's cap. "My clothing are in this bag; I'll just need to use the loo to change."

"Please help yourself, let me know if you need anything. I'll set up while you change." She closed the blinds and was adjusting the lighting when the phone rang.

"Hey Simone, what time are you coming over tonight? I want to try this new Italian place," said Nikki.

"Oh Nikki, sorry I totally forgot about dinner; I'll be busy for the next two hours, but I can take you out afterwards, it will be my treat."

"Simone...what's going on? Derrick just called and said an old grey-haired man walked into your studio after you closed. Are you on a date? If so, why are you keeping it a secret from me?"

Thomas reentered the room and stood still, quietly listened to the conversation.

"I'm not on a date, I'm with a friend who's helping me out with something," said Simone.

"Is that what they call it these days? What kind of help is your friend giving you? Derrick saw you hug and kiss the man."

"Nikki, tell your gossiping cousin to mind his own business. Why is he spying on me?"

"Ah excuse me," said Thomas, "I would be happy to take you and your friend out for dinner if it's alright with you. I was going to have dinner alone anyway." Simone spun around at the sound of Thomas's voice, not having realized he was out of the bathroom and able to listen to her call.

Simone covered the phone with her hand. "On one condition, you keep your disguise on until the end of the evening. Is that OK with you? I don't want my friend to bombard you with questions all night."

"That's perfect for me, I never know when Lemmings will show up," said Thomas. Simone returned to the phone, "I'll tell you what, Nikki, my grey-haired friend has just offered to take us out to dinner tonight, how would that be?"

"That would be perfect, it would give me the opportunity to get to know your 'friend.' What's his name anyway?"

"His name?" Simone said loudly, looking at Thomas.

Thomas whispered, "Oscar."

"His name is Oscar and we'll pick you up by seven twenty, so be ready. He doesn't like to be kept waiting."

"Oh, that's interesting, I can't wait to tell Derrick, bye."

"What, why tell Derrick?" said Simone but Nikki had already hung up.

"Is this Derrick your boyfriend?" asked Thomas.

"No, he's just my extremely nosy landlord and neighbor!" *I'd like to give him a piece of my mind,* Simone thought. *The nerve of him, calling Nikki to say I'm going out with a grey-haired man.* "He saw you hug me when you came in."

"Interesting, I have an idea; but before I forget, we have to postpone sessions for the next two weeks. The band and I have to do a video shoot and some recording in Mexico. We leave in two days."

"That's fine Thomas, I know you have work to do. Now, tell me your idea."

"I think we should give them something to talk about," said Thomas.

"I'm game. Why don't you sit into your pose and tell me your plans, 'Oscar,'" she said.

"Well to start, let's wrap up an hour early. You get ready

and I'll take you to my place. I'll exchange cars for one of the staff's SUVs, keep my grey hair and add a beard with mutton-chops. You can tell your friend I'm a landscaper, how does that sound?" said Thomas.

"The muttonchops might be overkill. Where should I say we met?" asked Simone.

"Let's say we met at one of your client's businesses? I was working on the landscape at the time, we struck up a conversation about gardening, and we hit it off and went out a few times. I volunteered to help with your yard today."

"What excuse could I use for not telling my best friend about you?"

"You could say you were embarrassed to tell your friends because I'm an old widowed grandfather."

Simone laughed. "Excellent, that would blow her mind! You're a very attractive grandfather, by the way."

"Oh, is my sweet young thing flirting with me now?" said Thomas as they both laughed.

Later that evening, after Thomas had added a mustache and goatee to his disguise, Thomas and Simone pulled up to Nikki's building. Spotting Nikki at the entrance, Simone exited the SUV and waved her over to them. Simone motioned for her to get into the back seat, but Nikki stopped at the front passenger window to look at the driver.

"Hello Oscar, my name is Nikki. It's nice to meet you."

Nikki extended her hand and Thomas shook it, saying, "It's a pleasure to meet you, darlin'" in a faux Irish accent. Simone shot him a look that said, *you're overdoing it*, but he continued: "We're going to a nice little Italian restaurant that I like; I hope you don't mind."

"Italian sounds great to me," said Nikki.

Thomas pulled up in front of Pelicci's a little after 7:30 PM.

Once inside, Thomas asked for reservations for Oscar and they were seated in a secluded booth in the back.

Nikki couldn't wait to start the questions. "So Oscar, I'm curious, how did you two meet?"

"It was by pure accident; I was managing a job for a client when Simone walked by and stopped to admire my azaleas. Seeing how much she enjoyed them, I was compelled to walk over and find out who she was; it was love at first sight." Thomas said this as he grasped Simone's hand in his and looked into her eyes. Simone stifled her chortle by giving him a kiss on the cheek. Thomas moved closer and put his arm around her shoulders.

"Oh, that sounds so sweet! When did all this happen?" asked Nikki.

"It was about three weeks ago; we try to meet any chance we get but our schedules are pretty hectic." Simone gave Thomas a small kick, hoping he would take the hint and stop talking. She could tell by the look on her friend's face that it was too late. After the waiter took their orders, Nikki excused herself to use the restroom, and asked Simone to come with her. Simone got up to leave, but before Thomas let her go, he pulled her close and kissed her on the lips. "Don't be too long sweetheart," he said. Nikki witnessed the exchange and chuckled to herself.

When the two entered the bathroom, Nikki looked around to make sure the stalls were empty before saying, "How dumb do you think I am? I had no idea you were at the kissing stage with Thomas! Why are you trying to keep this from me?"

Simone exhaled. "We weren't at any stage other than acquaintances. That was the first time he kissed me on the lips; guess he got carried away. I was going to tell you after dinner. What tipped you off?"

"Well, there are a list of things, the first is the wig; he

should have taken more time to secure it properly, it's just a little crooked. Obviously, you couldn't see it, being so close to him—or should I say on him. Second, the manicured nails don't belong to a landscaper, and third, he's Thomas Lloyd! I'd notice that face anywhere. You silly woman, why did you bring me on your date?"

"This isn't a date; I was working on his portrait and our dinner escaped my memory. When you called, Thomas offered to take us both out to dinner. I need three more sittings with him, so please don't tell anyone he comes to my studio, he's very fearful of paparazzi tracking him down."

"Did he dress as a chauffeur on one occasion?"

"Yes, how did you...? Derrick is an old gossip queen! He really needs to find a hobby."

"Simone, I think you *are* Derrick's hobby. The more I listen to him, the more it sounds like he has a thing for you," said Nikki.

"Listen, let's discuss this later, we've been in here a bit too long," said Simone.

Thomas was on his phone when they came back to the table. "You ladies were in there a while; I was just about to send a search party. I'll motion the waiter to come back; they were keeping the food warm."

"Sorry Thomas, it took a bit longer than we expected," said Simone. Thomas motioned with his eyes, clearly trying to tell her she'd called him by his real name. "And yes, Nikki knows who you are, she saw through your disguise. By the way, let me fix your hair." Simone reached up and moved the grey wig in place.

The waiter returned with their platters and sat them down. As the three prepared to eat, Simone said a short grace over her food.

Thomas watched her and wondered if he could have a relationship with a woman who put God in the middle of every-thing. Simone was unlike any other woman he'd been around. The conversations they'd had were the most enjoyable he'd had on any date. Well, he wished this was a date anyway. He wasn't sure how interested Simone was in him, but he'd made up his mind to find out soon. The only obstacle he could see was the landlord. He'd questioned Nikki about Derrick, and found out that he was her cousin. He mused that it would make sense for Nikki to encourage her friend to date her cousin; suddenly, he regretted the postponement of their sitting appointments.

Nikki continued asking Thomas a multitude of questions during their meal, and Thomas answered them all in stride, but he wished it was Simone asking the questions. He was attempt-ing to read Simone's thoughts when Nikki threw another one at him.

"So Thomas, does this mean I can get free tickets to your next concert?"

"Nikki!" Simone admonished.

"Tickets are not a problem, I'll send them to Simone for you," said Thomas. From experience, Thomas knew that Nikki was obviously fascinated by eating dinner with him, but Simone remained composed. Though he knew Simone was attracted to him—he could tell by the way her pulse had raced when he'd kissed her—he wasn't sure how she felt about him. Something told him that she was holding back her feelings, and Thomas hoped it had nothing to do with Derrick.

When everyone was done, the ladies thanked Thomas for dinner. Back in the truck, Thomas decided to drop Nikki off first, though Simone's home was closer. When they left Nikki at her door, she motioned for Simone to call her after Thomas turned around.

"Would you mind if I took you somewhere special before I drive you home?" asked Thomas.

"No, I don't mind, where are you taking me?" asked Simone.

"It's a surprise, but I'm sure you will enjoy it," Thomas said as he began to remove the wig and disguise from his face. They drove south for more than twenty minutes before coming to the entrance of Morden Hall Park. There were other people there, including children, all walking through the park's entrance. Some had flashlights or lanterns. Thomas parked the car and removed a blanket and flashlight from the trunk, then escorted Simone down the park's main path.

"This is very mysterious. Why are these people here; what's happening?" Simone asked.

"You will see soon enough, just be patient."

They walked into a great open field where people were finding spots on the grass, spreading their blankets, turning off their lights, and gazing upwards. Morden Hall Park was one of the few places in London where the sky was dark enough to stargaze, and Thomas loved coming to the park at night to look at the sky; the darkness was an added benefit that prevented others from recognizing him.

Tonight's sky was exceptionally. Earlier in the week, Thomas had read several stargazing blogs, all of which said tonight would be brilliant for gazing; the combination of dry days with clear skies and low moonlight offered the best stargazing environment. Thomas located a secluded spot on the field, spread out his blanket, and sat down with Simone. He gestured for her to lay flat on her back and look up as he did the same.

"Thom, this is wonderful! I never knew this park existed. Look, there's the Milky Way," said Simone as she pointed. Thomas liked that Simone had called him Thom, probably without realizing it. He reached out to take her hand in his, and he gazed upwards as he lay next to her. But his focus wasn't on the stars. Turning his head, he watched the delight on her face as she gazed into the sky. His heart kept prompting him to kiss her, but his mind couldn't foretell how she would react.

Later, when they left the park and arrived at Simone's home, Thomas purposely made extra noise with the car door. He slammed it closed, walked away, then came back and opened the door again as if he'd forgotten something, before slamming it again. As Thomas walked Simone to her door, he saw the light come on in the second-floor window next door. He waited until he saw the shadow of a head at the window before pulling Simone into his arms and kissing her intensely. He felt her welcoming response and continued the kiss.

"Good night Simone. I wish we didn't have to wait two weeks for our next session," he said before leaving. Simone was speechless, which was good; Thomas wanted Simone to have no doubts that he wanted more than her friendship; he also wanted Derrick to know that friendship was all he would have with her.

CHAPTER SEVEN
ACCESS

Thomas called Simone several times during the two-week period he was gone just to hear her voice; he couldn't wait to pick up where they'd left off. When the band went sightseeing in Mexico, Thomas sent Simone selfies with the group. He noted that she always seemed happy to hear from him, except for one Friday morning when her conversation seemed guarded. Thomas knew someone else was in the room when she spoke, and he hoped it was a customer. The next day, Simone received a huge bouquet of flowers with a note: *"You're on my mind and in my heart. Anxiously waiting to see you again."* When she called to thank him, she told him that she loved the flowers, and the attention, because he was on her mind everyday too.

It was the band's producer who had picked the distant Cabo San Lucas recording studio, but the bandmates loved the location; they worked on their tans in the morning then spent the rest of the day working in the studio. Though he also enjoyed the warm, sunny location, Thomas had hoped production would wrap up early so that he could get back to London ahead of schedule.

After noticing Thomas's frequent phone conversations with

Simone, his bandmates Alistair and Mick moved off to the side to have a whispered conversation. Alistair said, "This looks like the real deal; I've never seen Thom call a woman so often, usually *they're* badgering *him*."

"Is this the same woman who gave you guys a lift?" asked Mick.

"Yeah, she seems genuinely sweet; very focused on her career, not at all Thomas's type, but I believe he's smitten."

"That he is, I can tell by the new love ballad he wrote for the upcoming album. Well, if she's any better than Judy, he has my blessings," said Mick.

"Oh, please don't mention that bloody woman's name. She was toxic, and he was at her beck and call. Never knew what he saw in her."

"Yeah, that breakup was a blessing. And he's had a lengthy dry spell in the love department since rehab, so it's about time for him to get back on the horse," said Mick.

****

Once Access returned to London, the band stayed at their regular studio to re-work a few songs for the album before its completion; this had to be done quickly, because Access was booked to perform at the Hammersmith Apollo in London the next week. As promised, Thomas made sure Simone and Nikki had VIP packages that included front row seats and backstage passes.

On the day of their next painting appointment, Thomas confirmed that he would arrive early to take Simone to dinner before their painting session. This time, he took her to a French restaurant and arranged for a secluded booth. Simone saw that a few restaurant customers recognized Thomas when he entered, but he just casually waived at them while continuing to walk to the back with her. They sat side by side in a dark booth, and after the waiter left with their order, Thomas put his arm around her shoulder.

"Simone, it's been a very long two weeks; I couldn't wait to come back and do this," he said as he tilted her chin up and kissed her. Simone enjoyed the kiss that made her heart pound out of her chest, but when she opened her eyes, she realized he was watching her intently. Warning bells went off in her head because the look on his face told her that Thomas wanted more than a kiss tonight. It was an awkward moment; how could she push him away? But then she started second-guessing her instincts: *Maybe the look didn't mean what I thought it did?*

"I missed you too, Thomas. Now tell me all about your visit to Mexico," she said, hoping to change the subject. Thomas started talking about the shoot and some of the problems that had occurred, and after that Simone asked questions about his career. This remained the topic as they completed their meal, at which point she reminded Thomas that they had to return to the shop before it became too late to work on their project.

That night, Simone took extra time for the painting, and she estimated that one more session was needed to complete the portrait. It would have to wait until after the concert on Saturday. *And then what?* she thought. Could she stay in this relationship? She knew where Thomas wanted to take it, but she couldn't sleep with him. Her body wanted to, but she knew it was wrong—that it went against her faith.

****

On the night of the concert, Nikki came over early to inspect Simone's outfit. Ignoring her friend's protests, Nikki put away the outfit Simone had laid out; though Simone refused to wear the ensemble Nikki threw together—bright red leopard jeggings and a lace black faux bustier top she'd brought over. Simone had had her fill of fashion advice from her friend, so she pushed away Nikki's suggestion and put on what she'd originally planned to wear; skinny jeans, hot pink fashion high top sneakers, and a multicolored fashion tee with her leather jacket. She did take out her usual pony tail and brushed out her long auburn hair. Nikki changed her outfit to wear the red leopard jeggings that Simone had refused, and she also spiked her short blond hair and applied extra-long lashes along with her makeup.

Thomas had arranged for a limo to pick up them up an hour before the start of the concert. Nikki was very impressed with the ride, and she helped herself to the mini fridge and other freebie items in the back seat. When they arrived, the limo driver pulled up to a back doorway behind the Hammersmith, made a call, and waited with the motor running. A few minutes later, someone popped their head out the back door.

Speaking into the intercom, the driver said, "Ladies, if you look to your left, you will see a gentleman with a black shirt waving from the doorway. Please follow him, he will escort you to your seats. I will be here waiting after the concert to take you home." Impressed, the ladies thanked the driver and quickly exited the vehicle.

The man in the black shirt introduced himself as Roger and then led them through the service exit and down a few flights of stairs. Finally, they reached a doorway that opened to the front of the theatre seating.

"Ladies, the door we just exited will be locked during the concert, but after the band exits, I promise to come back, unlock the door, and bring you two backstage. Give me a few minutes though, OK?" said Roger. The women thanked him then went to find their front row seats. This was a first for Simone, she has never been in the front row of anything but school plays. After they took their seats, she looked around the theatre, noting that the venue was packed with fans.

Nikki tapped her shoulder. "Look at these other women in the front row, they're dressed like hookers. Look at that one, her breasts are pushed up so high they'll probably get cramps. This is why I wanted you to dress sexier; you can't let these women outshine you."

"Nikki, you just referred to these women as hookers, do you honestly want me to look like them?"

"Simone, you would be dressing for Thomas, and he *is* your boyfriend even though you're too shy to admit it."

"Nikki, what message would I be giving Thomas if I dressed like that? I'd be starting something with him that I couldn't finish. Let them wear whatever they like; I'm just here to enjoy the concert." Nikki sighed and tried to think of a way to prevent Simone from allowing Thomas to slip through her fingers.

Simone was loving the performance; she hadn't realized how great Thomas's vocals were. Being that her favorite mainstream artists were pop performers like Adele and Taylor Swift, she'd never been to a rock concert before. This week, she'd made a point of listening to all of Access's top hits. There were some surprising gems that she planned to keep in her playlist. Their music was mostly high-energy rock, though some songs had reggae beats, and a few were more like pop. At the concert, she watched in awe as Thomas worked the crowd into a frenzy.

Suddenly, the band started a new song with a slower pace, and Thomas began singing a love ballad. The other women on the front row were going mad with excitement; a few threw panties or bras at him, but Thomas wasn't fazed by it. He was clearly a pro who'd had a ton of underwear thrown at him over the years. As he was coming to the end of the ballad, Thomas looked directly at Simone. This didn't go unnoticed by the other front row women. A few of them looked her up and down, as if to say, *What's so special about her?* Simone didn't notice any of this because she was mesmerized by Thomas. Her heart was beating so loudly she wondered if Nikki could hear it.

Nikki watched Simone, whom she was certain didn't realize that she was glowing from Thomas's attention; now she had no doubt that her friend was in love.

After Access performed their last encore, Nikki and Simone stayed seated, waiting for Roger.

"Simone that was a great concert. Oh, you're so lucky!" whispered Nikki.

Simone eagerly anticipated seeing Thomas; though she imagine him being worn out after his performance. The band had played for more than two hours, and then returned for an encore performance.

Nikki nudged Simone out of her thoughts when she saw Roger at the door, motioning to them to come in. He brought them to a large lounge room that was set up with food and seating, and told them to help themselves. They could see the band talking and laughing through the window of the door at the end of the room.

A handful of various people were in the large room; one person was on a laptop, another was on the phone discussing another venue. *He must be their manager*, Simone thought. One guy came over and started talking to them about the concert sound. He introduced himself as Brian the sound engineer, and he was very entertaining. They were chatting with him for a while before the band members came out of the room to get food and drinks. Thomas immediately spotted them and walked over, saying hello to Nikki before putting his arm around Simone and kissing her.

"Why don't you ladies come in the room with the band."

He started moving in that direction with his arm still around her waist, so Simone and Nikki said goodbye to Brian.

The band members were scattered about the room. Mick was stretched out on the couch with a water bottle in his hand. Alistair was playing his guitar with headphones on. And two other band members had just exited the room.

Thomas slapped Mick on the knee to make him get up. "Hey Mick, I'd like you to meet some people. This is Simone and her friend Nikki."

"Hello," Mick said as he scooted over to one side of the couch to make room for them. Thomas sat with Simone on the other side of the sectional couch while Nikki sat in the middle. Alistair waved hello to Simone when he spotted her.

With his arm still around Simone, Thomas whispered in her ear, "Did you like the song I sung to you?"

Simone felt herself blushing as she smiled. "Yes, I loved the song and I loved that you sang to me," she said before Thomas kissed her. Alistair watched Thomas and thought he hadn't seen his friend like this in a long time. He couldn't remember any of Thomas's other girlfriends blushing before; and Simone seemed to be enjoying herself.

Suddenly the door burst opened, and Access's manager popped his head in to say, "Hey, it's time for you lot to go mingle with the VIP attendees a bit."

Thomas moaned as he slowly stood up. "This won't take long," he said to Simone and Nikki. "Why don't you ladies get something to eat and bring it back in here. We'll be back soon." Thomas and the other band members walked past the food buffet and down the hallway. Simone saw several camera flashes as the band neared the VIP section.

Nikki slid over with a grin on her face. "Wow Simone, Thomas couldn't keep his lips off you."

"Nikki, you're exaggerating. Let's go get something to eat."

After leaving the room, the two friends could hear Thomas and the rest of the band talking to their fans down the hall. Simone peeked around the corner and saw women hugging Thomas and taking selfies with him. She was sure it was innocent, but she reasoned that, if asked, these women would probably be happy to have sex with Thomas without question. *How can I compete with that?* "Nikki, am I doing the right thing?"

"What do you mean, Simone, why do you look so sad?"

"I don't think Thomas is the type to go without intimate relations with a girlfriend, and I know I can't do that with him. Am I setting us both up for heartbreak?"

"Hmm, I believe you should have this conversation with Thomas. You never know, he might surprise you."

The two friends waited for forty minutes before Simone took another look down the hallway. The band members were still surrounded by fans, signing autographs and posing for pictures. "Nikki, maybe we should go."

"What? Are you sure? I thought you and Thomas were having a great time."

"We were, but it looks like he may be tied up for a while. Besides, it's almost one in the morning."

"Aren't you going to tell him goodbye?" asked Nikki.

"He's busy with his fans now, I'll just send him a text," said Simone.

Nikki and Simone walked down the hallway in the opposite direction of the crowd, departing through an exit door where they were shocked by a bright camera flash from a photographer before they walked to the limo. The lone cameraman must have been waiting for the band, because he didn't seem excited about the surprise picture he'd just taken.

On their way home Nikki asked, "So what's next on the agenda for you two?"

"Well, we have one more painting session on Friday and that should be it."

"What do you mean? How can that be it? You two are in love."

"Nikki, you know me. We both know this relationship will end because I'm abstaining from sex until marriage."

"Simone, you're being so negative. You don't know if Thomas is like that. Give him a chance, he may 'honor your wishes.'"

"Nikki, did you see what I saw? Thomas is a great-looking rockstar who gets underwear thrown at him, and ladies to hug wherever he goes. A guy like that expects things."

"Simone, you're being unfair. Give him a chance; let him know where your boundaries are. He definitely loves you, everyone in the front row could see that, and you love him too. So just start from there and see what happens."

"I don't know, Nikki, the longer we're in this relationship, the harder it will be to let him go. Thomas might think I'm stringing him along, that I'm not taking his feelings into consideration."

****

The phone was ringing too early in the morning for Simone; she opened her eyes and saw that it was only five o'clock, two hours earlier than when she usually got up on Sunday to get ready for church services. It was Thomas calling. "Hi Thomas," she said groggily.

"Why did you leave me last night?" he asked abruptly.

"Sorry Thomas, you were busy, and I didn't think you would mind. I sent you a text."

"Yes, I received your text. I wish you'd told me in person that you were leaving. You could have at least given me a kiss goodbye."

"I think your fans had that covered," was her quick reply, but after saying it, she wished she could take it back. "Thomas, I didn't mean to say that. You know what, you're right. I should have said goodbye to you, I just wasn't sure if I should interrupt the session. Thomas, I'm running out of time, and I have to get ready for church now, I will see you at the last sitting on Friday, goodbye." Simone hung up before he could respond. She hated lying, but she'd wanted to end the conversation. Her thoughts were unsettled. She wanted to invite him over after church but decided against it because she didn't want to send the wrong signal. Nikki was right, they needed to have a talk about where this relationship was heading.

CHAPTER EIGHT
COLCHESTER

Thomas's disheartened demeanor made Simone anxious as she added the finishing touches to the portrait. She stepped back and examined the now-complete portrait intently with brush in hand, looking over every brushstroke to ascertain if more paint was needed. When she decided it was perfect and complete, she gestured to Thomas to come over to view his likeness.

"Simone this is fantastic. You've really captured my core, it's so much more than a photo."

"Thanks Thomas, I'm going to hang it in the window first thing in the morning. I'm sure everyone who comes in will ask about it."

"Now I wish I had a copy to hang it in my house," he said.

"I'll tell you what, after it's been on display for a year, I'll give it to you."

"Seriously? After all the work you've put into it?"

"Of course, it's your portrait, you sat for it, and I've had a great time."

"Well, grab your jacket, because we're going out to celebrate." Simone simply complied, while Thomas tried desperately to think of new ways for them to extend their time together.

They went to a Japanese restaurant for dinner. During the spectacular meal, the two had polite conversation, but Thomas noticed Simone was trying hard to avoid eye contact, and she seemed nervous.

"Before we leave, I wanted to ask you something. Would you mind coming with me to Colchester tomorrow morning, if you don't already have plans? It's a charming town, filled with historical sites, and very picturesque. You could take some great photos there."

"That sounds nice. Are you going for business? Do you need me to help you with anything?"

"No, just bring yourself, I'd love the company. I do have business there that I check on every now and then. Would it be OK for me to picked you up at 10 AM?"

"10 is perfect, I promise to be ready this time."

As they entered the car to go back to Simone's home, Simone knew she needed to discuss ending their relationship, but she didn't know how to start the conversation. The feelings she had for him were so strong, and the last thing she wanted to do was disappoint Thomas.

When she gave her life to Christ, it meant no premarital sex. Thomas was an agnostic, who by his own account, had slept with many women. But she couldn't and wouldn't engage in casual sex. Her mind told her this was not a good situation to be in because of the strong feelings she felt for Thomas, but her heart loved those strong feelings, and the man himself.

Thomas wasn't the first person she'd dated since coming to London; however, she'd felt almost nothing for the other men. They were nice guys, but she knew what love felt like, and she did not have those feelings for them. In her heart, she knew that this was an issue she should go to God in prayer about, but she'd been longing for someone for so long, and Thomas was wonderful to her. How could she end this relationship? *There must be another way*, she thought.

They'd been parked outside of Simone's home for a few minutes now, and Thomas watched Simone in silence because she was so heavy in thought she hadn't realized the car was stopped. When he leaned over and kissed her on the lips, it was a slow, patient, loving kiss. Simone instinctively wrapped her arms around his shoulders to pull him closer. Her movement only encouraged his hands to travel over her body, but the sound of Thomas's moan woke her out of the passionate trance. Abruptly, she broke away from the kiss, grabbed her bag, and quickly exited the car. She stooped down and said, nervously, "Goodnight, I'll see you in the morning," before quickly walking to her door.

Thomas couldn't reply because he had to catch his breath. He couldn't understand why Simone had run out of the car, away from him. He'd felt her desire in the kiss; she'd put her arms around him, he knew he hadn't imagined it, so why had he seen fear in her eyes?

Inside her home, Simone set her keys down and picked up the phone to call Nikki before she got ready for bed. Her friend knew she was going out after completing the portrait, and she was waiting for Simone's call. "Hi Nikki, I'm back."

"Humph, you called me a lot sooner than I wanted you to. So, Ms. Mills, tell me, how deep is your love!"

"Nikki, it's not that serious, we just kiss."

"Simone, I've seen you two kiss. I can tell Thomas is serious. What I want to know is if it's serious for you."

"I know you think I should pursue a relationship with Thomas, but you know my position."

"Simone, I'm certain there are many Christians out there having premarital sex."

"That may be true, those relationships do exist, but the rule is there to protect us. I'm supposed to flee from temptation, and Thomas is very tempting. I don't want to lead him on."

"I think you really should give this relationship a chance. You shouldn't give up on Thomas because of what you imagine he thinks. Talk to him, allow him to decide if he doesn't want to date you. Besides, no one is perfect, not even Christian men. I've read that some Christian men have porn problems, am I right?"

"Yes, I've heard that too. Listen, I'm not looking for a perfect man. I know that doesn't exist. But a real Christian man would, and should, understand that you want marriage before sex. The non-Christian man will laugh at that lifestyle."

"That's true Simone, but it's also true that you've dated Christian men and nothing has come of those relationships. Before doing anything rash, you must tell him how important your faith is."

"That's so easy to say now when I'm speaking with you, but when I'm looking into those blue eyes, everything leaves my head and I can't focus on anything."

"Oh Simone, sounds like you've got it bad. Sweetheart, you know you love him; don't throw this relationship away. Who knows if you'll ever feel this way for anyone again."

"Thomas asked me to travel with him to Colchester tomorrow morning. I said yes, but now I think I should cancel."

"Simone, I know you try to focus only on your business, but you're a beautiful woman—on the inside and out. People see it, Derrick sees it—a beautiful woman who's not living her life to the fullest. Go to Colchester, have a good time, then let him know who you are and take it from there."

****

Thomas was prompt. He called her from the car to let her know that he was outside. When she met him there, she found that today he drove a Land Rover. Simone was ready for the drive; she'd dressed in jeans, light walking shoes, a thick, warm sweater, and a light jacket. The sun was out, but the November winds were blowing hard. She'd brought a small crossover handbag along with her camera case.

After she got in the car, Thomas said good morning; then he leaned over and kissed her on the lips so casually you'd think they did it all the time. Simone said nothing as her mixed feelings arose again.

During the drive, Thomas pointed out different landmarks, many of which Simone never knew of. After about eighty minutes, they arrived at an Italian restaurant.

"Are you ready for an early lunch?" he asked.

"Sure, I don't mind," she said. Once inside, Simone studied the décor. It had a Tuscan feel with a modern twist that somehow went together well. All the staff greeted Thomas by name as he escorted her to a secluded table at the back of the restaurant.

"Stay here and order what you want. I have a little business to take care of, and then I'll be right out." While he was gone, their waiter came and took her order. When the food arrived, the waiter set down a plate for Thomas too. Soon after, Thomas returned to the table. "How do you like your food?" he asked.

"It's very good, and fresh. Do you own this restaurant?"

"Yes, this is one of my investments. I figure at some point I may not want to tour anymore, and I'll need something else to keep me busy."

"Why do you say that? Don't you love to sing?"

"Oh yes, I love to sing, but there are so many other unpleasant aspects to the work I do that you don't see. Most people think the life of a musician is very exciting, and to be honest, when we start a tour it is, but we travel so much to mostly the same cities on every tour. It becomes routine; sometimes, you just want to be at home. You have to promote yourself during the tours. That means you have to give early morning interviews, be guests on shows, and attend autograph events. Deal with problems like staff members allowing unauthorized women in your room. On top of it all, you have to avoid speaking too much so you can conserve your vocals for the concert. All these things take away from the joy of performing."

"I never thought of it that way. I guess most people focus on the thousands of adoring fans shouting 'I love you' all night long," she teased.

Thomas laughed but became serious as he looked at her. "I would give anything to hear you shout that to me," he said. Simone looked down to avoid his gaze.

"Simone, tell me what's going on, why you looked away? I know you have feelings for me, and I'm sure you know how I feel about you. We are two adults, and I want to be with you." He reached out to tilt her face towards him and said, "Simone, from the first night I looked at you in your car, I wanted to see you again. What's wrong? Am I coming on too strong for you? It seems whenever we get close, you run away from me. Tell me what I'm doing wrong?" Simone was speechless. "Please, tell me how you feel; what is the issue between us? Is it Derrick?" he asked.

"No, this has nothing to do with Derrick, we're just friends. I'm sorry Thomas, maybe I shouldn't have come here with you. It has to do with my faith and my past. I can't do what you want me to do because it's against who I am. I know this sounds strange to you, but my faith doesn't permit premarital sex. I have been agonizing over how to tell you, and I'm completely stressed because, yes, I do like you, but I also feel guilt and anxiety when I'm with you. My mind tells me I shouldn't be here; I should have said no, but at the same time my heart can't say no to you. I'm sorry, I haven't been fair to you and I should have said something earlier, but I could never get the words out, especially when you're looking at me."

"Let me see if I understand this correctly; you're telling me we can't be together because God doesn't like agnostics?"

"That's not what I'm saying. And I'm definitely not saying God doesn't like you—God loves everyone, even the people who don't follow Him. But when a person chooses to follow Him, it means living a life that glorifies Him. And one way to do that is waiting until marriage for sex."

"Simone I'm confused, you're doing my head in, but I believe you said you have feelings for me, is that correct?"

"Yes, Thomas I do have feelings for you."

"Good, let's leave this restaurant and enjoy the remainder of the day. I'd rather continue this conversation later in privacy, is that alright with you?"

"Yes, that's fine with me," Simone said.

After leaving the restaurant, they drove through the small town to Colchester Castle for sightseeing. Later, Thomas took Simone to the elevated countryside so she could shoot some pictures. From the car, Simone viewed many picturesque areas to photograph, but Thomas promised her the best areas were further up on the walking trail in High Woods Country Park. He parked the Range Rover at the park's entrance, and as Simone exited the car, she could see why Thomas had said this was the best location for photographs. From their vantage point, she saw beautiful glens and meadows in the distance. Every view looked like a postcard.

Simone began walking along the ridge to get a better view of the lower valley, and Thomas came up behind her as she started snapping photos. "Looks like we won't have as much time as I thought, there are some heavy rain clouds headed this way. We should leave soon," he said.

"I guess I'll have to hurry then." Simone hiked further down the ridge to take more pictures.

"Simone be careful, some of that ground doesn't look stable."

"Thomas I'll be fine; I've hiked before, you know. I used to hike on the Appalachian Mountain trails in New York whenever I got the chance. With the clouds rolling in from a distance, these pictures should turn out great." She glanced back at Thomas and noted the worried expression on his face. Simone quickly snapped a few shots of him before continuing along the ridge, which grew more rugged after the shallow path ended. Huge shrubs and tall grasses obstructed her hike. As she walked around one large shrub, St. Botolph's Priory ruins came into view. They were breathtaking from this distance. The eleventh-century Augustinian ruins stood out from the modern buildings surrounding the area. Simone adjusted her zoom lens and began snapping. She was walking through a group of stones to get a better shot, but the loose soil under the stones gave way, causing her to slide down the ridge for a few seconds before she was able to stop herself. Grateful she hadn't dropped her camera, Simone stood to turn back. As her foot touch the ground, pain radiated from her heel.

Thomas came up behind her. "Simone, are you hurt?"

"No I'm fine. I just hit my foot on a stone. It doesn't hurt that much," said Simone.

"I think you meant to say yes then," said Thomas as he examined her foot. "You have an abrasion and a small gash. It's bleeding. Let me help you up."

"Thomas I'm fine, I'll meet you back at the car in a few minutes." Simone waited until Thomas walked away before she started snapping more pictures. A few minutes passed before she decided she had taken enough photos, and then Simone slowly limped her way back around the shrubs, the pain in her foot increasing as she walked on it.

Already in the car, Thomas checked the rearview mirror, expecting to see Simone, but she wasn't in view. Shaking his head, Thomas exited the vehicle to track her down. When he turned to enter the trail, the rain clouds opened up, instantly converting the dry dirt trail into mud puddles. Thomas ran back along the ridge until he saw Simone running with a limp. He quickly scooped her up and ran for the car, though they were drenched when they reached the Land Rover. Thomas took a blanket from the trunk and draped it around Simone. Then got back in the car and drove carefully down the steep gravel lane until they reached the main road. Going in the opposite direction from where they came, he made several turns until he reached a small road that led to a long, mostly obscured driveway.

The rain still poured when Thomas parked in front of a cottage entryway. He ran to the passenger side, scooped up Simone, and sprinted to the front door of his Colchester home. Once inside, he put Simone down on the stone floor before turning on the fire place. "I'm going to change in my suite; there's a bathroom next to the bedroom down the hall. You'll find some towels and bandages in there. I'm sure you can also find some robes and sleepwear in the bedroom closet," he said.

Simone was chilled to the bone. She found the bathroom, peeled off her wet clothes, and hopped into a hot shower. When she got out, she wrapped a towel around her torso before applying peroxide and bandages to her bleeding foot. The décor in the bedroom next door was definitely feminine, and the closet was filled with women's clothing. Simone wondered who they belonged to as she selected a fluffy warm robe with a matching gown and put them on.

As she walked back to the great room, she noticed her bloody footprints on the floor. "Sorry Thomas, I made your floor look like a crime scene. Where do you keep your mop?"

"Don't worry about it, I'll set the robotic mop to take care of that," he said.

"Well at least allow me to make the tea," said Simone.

"I don't believe I can trust you with that, you Americans aren't known for making tea," he joked.

"Oh, how hard is it to drop a tea bag into a cup of water?"

"Tea bag! Are you serious?"

"My goodness, you're so old-fashioned Thom."

"I'll tell you what, why don't you get something to cover your bandaged foot. If you go to my suite on the left you'll see a tall wardrobe, there should be some athletic socks in the bottom drawer."

"Thanks," she said as she walked to the room.

"When you return, I'll have a real cup of tea for you."

Simone rolled her eyes in response.

"I saw that," Thomas yelled as he watched her limp down the hallway.

In the suite, Simone opened the drawer and pulled out a pair of thick woolly long socks. After putting them on, she turned around and admired the bedroom. There was a massive four-poster bed in the middle of the room with a nail-studded grey suede headboard against a brick wall. On the wall opposite the massive ornate wooden wardrobe was a huge full-length antique mirror. She enjoyed the feel of the plush royal blue carpet under her feet. Simone imagined the tall bed being extremely comfortable; that thought made her leave the room quickly.

Back in the kitchen, Thomas had teacups prepared next to

a picnic basket. "I'd brought the picnic basket thinking that we could eat dinner out in the countryside, but my kitchen will have to do," he said.

"I love how you've designed the rooms of your house; you've got great taste," Simone said.

"Thanks, but everything you see was designed by my mother. She stays here sometimes; those were her things in the closet where you found the robe. I've put your wet clothes in the washer/dryer combo, they should be ready in a bit."

"Thanks Thomas."

They were finishing up their meal when Simone's phone rang, and she hurried to get it out of her handbag.

"Hi Mom."

"Hi Simi, where are you? I called your home earlier and left a message."

"I'm having dinner with a friend."

"That's nice, what type of restaurant did you go to?"

"Actually, we're eating at my friend's house."

"You mean you're at Nikki's?"

"No, not Nikki, a new friend."

"What's your new friend's name?"

"His name is Thomas; I did some painting for him."

"Simone, are you on a date? That's wonderful."

"Mom it's not like that; don't get so excited."

"Alright Simi, I understand you don't want to talk about it. I was calling to see if you're definitely not coming for Thanksgiving. Everyone will be so disappointed if you're not here."

"No Mom, nothing's changed. I can't come for Thanksgiving. I have to generate as much business as possible before the Christmas season. I promise you I'll be all yours for the week of Christmas though."

"OK, I miss you Simi."

"I miss you too Mom. I can't wait to come home to see you. Tell Martin he'd better be there when I come."

"Will do sweetie, I love you."

"I love you too Mom, goodbye."

"Sorry Thomas, that was my mom checking up on me," she said.

"I'm not sorry, I like knowing more about you," he said.

Simone dreaded having to have this conversation, but she knew it was time. "Thomas, we have to talk," she started.

"Wait, I know what you're going to say, but I don't want to hear it because I still want to do this." He quickly moved over and kissed her. Simone instinctively kissed back—but, acutely aware of where she was, and what she wasn't wearing, she quickly stepped back.

" I...I think I should put my clothes on now." Simone ran to the machine, took her clothes out, and headed for the bedroom to change. Chastising herself, she made up her mind to go home, and though she hated to think about it, end this relationship before it went too far.

This situation was new to Thomas; he didn't know what to do, or say. No woman had ever said no to him before. Knowing that Simone wasn't the type of woman to be swayed by jewelry or sweet-talk, he racked his brain, trying to figure out a way to prolong their relationship. When Simone returned, she found Thomas in the same spot, deep in thought. Simone put her hand on his shoulder, "Thomas, I need to go home now."

He sighed deeply. "I wanted you to stay, but I guess you're right. We aren't working out, and I go on tour next month anyway. Seems a shame to end us like this though. Wait, you're not going to your Thanksgiving holiday next week, why don't you let me host a Thanksgiving dinner for you before I leave? We can have it on the Friday after your Thanksgiving holiday. You can invite Nikki and I'll invite Alistair and his wife, Cynthia.

I'll also invite Mick; I think he sort of likes Nikki. Then we can end our relationship as friends."

"That sounds really nice of you, Thom, but you don't have to do that for me. Besides, what do you know about the Thanksgiving meal?" she said.

"Hey, isn't it just a glorified English Christmas dinner?" he answered.

"You couldn't be more wrong. You're basically insulting me right now," Simone said jokingly. "OK, it sounds like a good plan, what should I bring?"

"I don't want you to bring anything but yourself. Just come and let me surprise you. What do you say?"

"I don't want you to go to so much trouble, let me do something," said Simone. Thomas continued to refuse her help.

Soon after, they left the house and headed back to London. When Simone arrived home, she called Nikki and told her everything that had happened, including the Thanksgiving dinner invite.

"Simone, I still don't understand this. You love him and he loves you, are you sure you're doing the right thing?"

"Nikki I'm human. I love everything about Thomas, and I love spending time with him, but Thomas wants more than kisses, and I can't give in. You have no idea how hard it is for me to walk away. After all these years, I've finally fallen in love again, and now I have to give it up." Suddenly tears streamed down her cheeks.

"I'm so sorry Simone, I didn't mean to upset you. Are you just going to say goodbye on Friday and never see him again?"

"I'm saying goodbye to the relationship, and being close friends won't work because we're too attracted to each other; so, yes, I don't plan to see Thomas again."

CHAPTER NINE
THANKSGIVING

The following week was very busy for Simone, in part because the display of Thomas's portrait in the window brought many new customers into her shop. Most were just curious, but she received several orders from patrons for painted portraits. These customers didn't like the idea of multiple sittings, so Simone compromised with one long session and plans to complete the portraits using photographs taken at the sitting. It wasn't the same as a complete personal portrait, but it was close enough. These were for Christmas presents, so she would need to complete all of them before she left for New York.

Derrick stopped bringing coffee on Fridays, and it actually seemed as though he wasn't speaking to her at all. Occasionally, Simone would spot him peeking in her window; however, there was always a displeased expression on his face, and he never stepped in to speak. She missed their friendship and wished things could go back to the way they were.

The Friday after Thanksgiving came quickly. That morning, Simone woke up early, beginning her work day at 5 AM to take care of as much business as possible so she wouldn't run late for Thomas's dinner that evening, which was set to start at 6 PM. Simone's hectic day began with multiple Christmas card photo requests. Most were of little children and infants who always took extra time for positioning; they tired her out before the work day was over. Luckily, Nikki was driving directly to Thomas's house, so that saved Simone time from picking up her friend and drop her back home afterwards.

After closing the studio an hour early, Simone took a quick shower and shampooed her hair. Her usual ponytail didn't feel appropriate for her and Thomas's last evening as a couple so Simone dried her long hair and took time to style it into cascading curls. She dressed in black pumps, a burgundy sateen circle skirt, and a light grey patterned cashmere sweater under her jacket.

In spite of what Thomas had said about not bringing anything, Simone had made a batch of carrot nog, a holiday drink she'd learned to make from Marcy's mother. When Simone had tasted her first glassful, she'd sworn traditional egg nog would never touch her lips again. This creamy nog contained no eggs, but it was rich, smooth, and full of flavor. It had been a staple at her family's holiday celebrations since her first time making the beverage at home. To make it, she first juiced fresh carrots, then she mixed the juice with cinnamon, freshly grated nutmeg, vanilla, honey, half and half, and Irish Cream liqueur. With her gift in hand, Simone arrived twenty minutes early, hoping to assist Thomas or determine if any of his dishes needed help.

Thomas opened the door and said, "You look wonderful; I love what you did with your hair."

"Hi Thomas, I came early to see if you needed help." As Thomas moved aside to let her in, he inhaled the sweet scent of her freshly shampooed hair and admired her locks as she walked by.

"This is for you, it's carrot nog."

"Thanks, but I said not to bring anything."

"I know, but I feel funny arriving empty-handed. Is something burning?" she asked.

"Oh no," said Thomas, taking off to the kitchen; but it was too late, the mashed potatoes were scorched.

"Thomas, are you doing the cooking yourself? I thought you would have asked Libby."

"Libby did do the cooking; my job was to warm up the mashed potatoes," he said dejectedly.

Simone laughed and said, "You need some help. Why don't you put the carrot nog with the other beverages and give me the apron; I'll take over from here."

"Are you sure? It doesn't seem right since you're the guest of honor," said Thomas.

Simone was already in the refrigerator, looking for replacement potatoes. "Don't worry, just show me where everything is, then you can leave and take care of your guests."

Simone rinsed, peeled, and quartered the replacement potatoes. She then quick-cooked them in the microwave while getting half and half, butter, and seasonings ready. Simone checked on the other foods warming in the ovens and found a stuffed turkey, ham, green beans, rolls, cranberry sauce, and, surprisingly, two pumpkin pies.

She heard voices in the dining room before Nikki came in to hug and greet her.

"Simone, this house is gorgeous, and you look spectacular, even in an apron. How are you doing in here, do you need my help? Thomas said you were helping him with an emergency."

"Hi Nikki, no thanks, the emergency is over. I've made a new batch of mashed potatoes and everything else is ready."

Thomas entered the kitchen. "Ok, it's time for you to be a guest again so I'm kicking you out of the kitchen. You too, Nikki. By the way, that carrot nog is fabulous." Simone removed her apron and walked with Nikki into the sitting room. Alistair came over to say hello, introducing them to his wife, Cynthia. She was tall like Alistair but with long light-brown hair.

"Simone was our hero, she's the one who rescued us from the paparazzi," said Alistair.

"Alistair told me all about that. Weren't you afraid of those aggressive photographers?" asked Cynthia.

"No, I was just tired and angry. I wanted to go home, but those photographers would not move out of the road. They sat like vultures around their small sports car, I felt sorry for whoever was trapped inside. That's when I got the idea to do a drive-by rescue."

Thomas came into the room and announced, "Dinner is served," and all the guests stood and followed Thomas into the large dining room. In there, he had set the food on a buffet against the dining room wall with the serving dishes on warmers.

"Thomas, I'm very impressed, you did a great job," said Simone. The other guests also complimented him on the arrangement.

"If no one minds, I'd like to say grace before we eat—it's customary in the US," Simone said, watching Thomas's face closely. The guests seemed in agreement so she proceeded. "Dear Lord, we thank You for providing this meal that we are partaking of. Please bless those who've provided it and Lord we also ask that You keep those who are travelling abroad safe and secure. We ask this in Jesus's name. Amen." Everyone around the table said Amen. Cynthia complimented Simone on her prayer.

All proceeded to the buffet, made their plates, and sat at the table; Thomas and Simone sat next to each other. Libby had decorated the table with a wrought iron candelabra set in vines of holly. The candelabra held large ivory candle pillars. Small orange gourds, red apples, and grapes were also included in the arrangement.

"Thomas, I love this tablescape, it's gorgeous," stated Simone.

Thomas brought out several bottles of the wine that Simone liked. He teased her by saying, "Of course, only an American would fall in love with an American wine." Thomas kept everyone's wine glass filled, and everyone seemed to be in good spirits. In conversation, Simone found out that Cynthia was a member of an Anglican church. Though Alistair wasn't a member, at his wife's request, he attended with their children every Christmas and Easter.

After their meal, Thomas served the pumpkin pies, which Simone thought were surprisingly good considering the dish is not common in England, though Thomas was adamant that pumpkin pie wasn't for him.

"Thomas, how do you know that you don't like it if you've never tried it?" asked Simone.

"But it's squash, how good can squash pie taste?" said Thomas.

Simone sliced a small piece with his fork and put it to his mouth before saying, "Please just try it once for me."

He took the bite and moved the forkful around in his mouth. "It's not as bad as I thought it would be," he said. Simone continued to hand feed him small bites, and though Thomas thought the pie was just OK, he continued to eat because he enjoying being fed by Simone. Nikki smiled to herself as she watched them from across the table.

Alistair protested, "Simone, are we allowed to have music at Thanksgiving? It's very quiet in here."

"Music is fine. In the US the men usually watch a football game or some other sport after dinner."

"Well, I wouldn't mind watching some football, but I don't think Cynthia would allow me to. Oh, there she goes, she's shaking her head no. Ok, we'll listen to some music." Alistair selected some Harry Connick Jr. and John Legend tracks to play before he pulled Cynthia up to dance. Thomas stood up and held out his hand to Simone, who gladly joined him.

Mick, who was dressed in a blazer and ascot, looked at Nikki and said, "We can't just sit here and watch them dance. Come on, let me show you my moves." Nikki laughed and stood up to dance with him.

****

It was after ten o'clock when Alistair and Cynthia said their goodbyes. Nikki thanked Thomas and said her goodbyes too before walking to her car with Mick. Not wanting to leave just yet, Simone decided to stay behind and help Thomas clean up. He was about to protest, but then remembered that this was their last day as a couple, and instead thanked her for staying longer.

Simone's feet began to ache, reminding her that she'd been up since 5 AM, and she removed her shoes and got to work on the dishes. After finishing, she cleaned the kitchen and dining room; the food was put away and all the plates were stacked in the cabinet. Finally, Simone collapsed on the sofa next to Thomas, who was watching TV.

"Simone, you shouldn't tire yourself out, you didn't have to do all of that," he said.

"It was the least I could do. Thank you for giving me a great Thanksgiving dinner. I didn't realize how much I'd miss it until the day came and went. This gathering helped a great deal."

"Simone, I'd do anything to make you happy. Here, why don't you drink some wine and relax your feet." She took the glass of wine from Thomas and relaxed her head on the over-stuffed couch. Thomas proceeded to lift her feet to his lap.

"Thomas, what are you doing?"

"I'm checking on your foot. Are you in pain? Has your injury healed well?" he asked.

"Oh yes, it's fine; I took my shoes off because I've been on my feet since very early in the morning; they're just a little achy now." Thomas started to massage both feet. "Thomas, that feels so good, where did you learn to do that?"

"After my dad died, my mother had no choice but to work long hours in the store. The first thing she'd do after walking in the house was remove her shoes; then she'd rest a few minutes before getting up. I watched her rub her feet so often that eventually I just started doing it for her so she could relax."

"You're a good son, Thomas." Simone put down the glass of wine and decided to shut her eyes for a minute before getting ready to go home.

Thomas watched Simone doze off, waiting until she was motionless for more than fifteen minutes before he retrieved a blanket to place over her. Sitting on the edge of the couch watching her chest rise and fall, he wondered how to say goodbye to a woman he wanted to stay in his life. Knowing that it was their last time together, he leaned over her body and gently pressed his lips to hers. Simone's arms unexpectedly rose and wrapped around his back. This act turned the simple kiss into a passionate one that encouraged him to place his arm under her knees. Then, without breaking their connection, Thomas gently lifted Simone into his arms and carried her to his bedroom.

CHAPTER TEN
SATURDAY

Simone stretched before opening her eyes, noting that there was a weight on her back. Her now-open eyes didn't register where she was until she turned around and saw Thomas, still asleep, with his arm resting on her back. In an instant, memories of their night together flooded her mind. She recalled everything they'd done; however, the recollections came with instant regret.

Simone moved slowly to ease Thomas's arm off her back without waking him. Once out of bed, she grabbed her clothes off the floor and left the room as quickly as possible. A few doors away from Thomas's bedroom Simone discovered a full bath. After a quick shower, she searched for and located her shoes in the living room, then quietly exited the house, all before 7:30 AM.

Simone walked quickly to her car and drove off, never noticing the man standing just outside the gate, snapping pictures of her every move. Completely distracted, her thoughts were only of last night. Simone couldn't figure out how she'd gotten into Thomas's bed, but what she'd done willingly in it filled her with anxiety and guilt.

Somehow, in spite of her preoccupied thoughts, she

reached her home safely. As she exited the car, her eye caught Derrick peeking from his window. Sighing to herself, she realize that Derrick would tell all the neighbors that she'd come home early in the morning. Once inside, Simone undressed and took another shower. Afterwards, while she dressed, her business phone rang, and her hand froze midair upon seeing Thomas's number displayed. She let the call go to voicemail and was not surprised when a few minutes later a voicemail symbol popped up on her cellphone screen. She played it immediately.

"*Hey, it's Thom. I woke up and you weren't here. Why didn't you wake me before you left? I miss you already. Please call me when you get in.*"

Simone really needed to speak to someone about what had happened. Nikki picked up after the first ring.

"*Simone? Whoa, what time did you get in last night? I called at midnight but you didn't answer.*"

"Nikki, I did something terrible. It happened, I don't know how it started, but I slept with Thomas last night, and I'm so angry with myself. I should have left when you did."

"*Simone, how did that happen?*"

"I don't know. After cleaning up I remember lying on the sofa. Thomas gave me a glass of wine and started massaging my feet. I closed my eyes for a few minutes, I must have fallen asleep... I remember we kissed...and I could have stopped, but I didn't."

"*Simone, it's alright, your relationship was headed in that direction, that's why you wanted to break it off. Don't beat yourself up about it, you slipped up once, try not to worry about it. What did Thomas say when you left?*" asked Nikki.

"Ummm... I sort of left before he got up."

"*Oh Simone, you didn't! That's a terrible thing to do, did you at least call him? Simone, you can't just walk away and not communicate."*

"I know, I know, he left a message on my phone; I'll call him back later."

"What are you going to say, are you still going to end your relationship?"

"I have to, now more than ever; the temptation is too great. This is why I should have ended the relationship sooner."

"Listen, you're both single, surely something could be worked out."

"Nikki, Thomas isn't interested in celibacy, and he doesn't care about my beliefs; working it out would put me at risk of having sex with him again. I was careless last night, but I won't allow myself to be alone with him again."

"I understand, but before you write him off, you must talk to him. At least let him know you're home."

"I will. I'll call him back this morning, I promise. Wait— Nikki, someone's buzzing my door, let me call you back." Simone ended the call and ran to unlock the shop door. Expecting a customer unfamiliar with her shop's opening hours, she swiftly opened the door, ready to let them know she was closed. Instead, it was Thomas who stood before her. He came in and promptly closed the door behind him. Just standing close to him brought back memories of being in his arms last night. She didn't want eye contact; however, Thomas grasped her shoulders, forcing Simone to face him.

"Simone, you left without saying anything. I called several times from the car, and every call went to voicemail, yet you're here."

"I'm sorry Thomas, I had to leave. I actually should have left last night with Nikki."

"I'm glad you didn't. Simone last night was wonderful and

I know you enjoyed it too." He moved to embrace her but Simone stepped aside and looked away.

"Thomas, I can't let this happen again."

"What are you saying? Are you telling me we can't be together because of your beliefs, or is it something else—or someone else?"

"What are you talking about?"

"I'm talking about the man who watches my every move whenever I come to your door, Derrick. There is something going on between you, isn't there?"

"No, there was never anything going on between us. We'd only have coffee on Friday mornings before work."

"Just the two of you?"

"Yes—sometimes we talk about current events, sometimes he talks about the other tenants. It's just coffee!"

"Simone, either you're hiding the truth or you're oblivious to his feelings. The looks he gives me says your Friday mornings are about more than coffee."

"Thomas, you're the only man I've slept with since my freshman year at college; there are no other romantic relationships in my life. And last night was my mistake, it never should have happened. That's my fault, not yours, I'm the one who has to stay celibate. You think this was a good thing, but I'm so ashamed of myself, of what I did; it's weighing on me, and I don't want to feel this way."

"Simone, there's nothing to be ashamed of. We had sex because we're two people who are in love with each other. You have no control over who you fall in love with and neither do I; what I do know is, once you find someone, you don't throw them away as if they mean nothing."

"I never said you meant nothing to me. That's the problem: you mean too much. This is very hard for me, but you have to understand that I can't live the lifestyle you want for me. I'm sorry, our relationship has to end now." Thomas grabbed her waist and kissed her but Simone pushed him away. "You have to leave. Now," she said without looking up at him.

Shaking his head as he watched the woman who'd slept in his arms only a few hours ago cry. Thomas released a heavy sigh. Knowing that nothing he could say would change Simone's mind, he did as she'd requested and left.

CHAPTER ELEVEN
THOMAS

Thomas hurried out to the airport parking lot, grimacing against the damp wind as he ran across the tarmac towards the band's private jet. Though he'd gone to bed early the night before, sleep did not come until the morning hours. Oversleeping was so out of character for him, and it had happened today of all days. This tour was supposed to be his main focus.

Simone had dominated his thoughts all night, and he was determined to not waste any more time on his failed relationship, so he'd brought sheet music and his laptop along to occupy his thoughts during the long flights.

Shaking his head, Thomas saw the irony in his situation. He was the one who typically ended relationships. Even before the band hit the big time, women were all over him; they were disposable. Sometimes he couldn't even remember their names when they called.

My Simone, the woman who lives like a nun. I mean, who goes nine years without sex? I should have expected her to dump me. How can a woman like that want to live with an aging recovering addict? If only those idiots had allowed me to drive away. I never would have heard her voice or looked into those large green eyes. I do feel a little guilty for sleeping with her, though I don't regret that it happened. Her eyes had a bewildered look at first, but then she reached up and kissed me while her other hand pulled me closer. Afterwards, when she fell asleep in my arms, it felt so right; like she was mine and meant to be there with me.

How does a woman go from making sweet, passionate love all night, to cutting off the relationship hours later? She was hard on herself, though, like she fell short of her own standards.

Maybe Simone will come to her senses while I'm away. I know she wants to be with me; I could feel it; but she has options, doesn't she? There's good ole Derrick who conveniently lives next store, the guy who's "just a friend." Wish there was some way I could keep them apart; but how, and would it do any good if I'm not enough for her anyway?

There's Alistair looking out the jet door, I'll never hear the end of it if I'm the last one in. "Where's Mick?" asked Thomas.

"Mick's already snoring in his seat, we're all here waiting on you," said Alistair.

"Sorry about that, sort of got caught up and lost track of time."

"Oh, you mean you were caught up with Simone," said Alistair.

"No, you've got the wrong idea. It's not what you think," said Thomas.

"Are you telling me you weren't *visiting* with Simone?"

"I wish I were mate, but no, I just overslept."

"Are you putting me on? From the way you two were looking at each other on Friday, I'm surprised she's not coming on tour with us," said Alistair.

Thomas just shrugged as he buckled his seatbelt and turned on his headphones to avoid continuing the conversation with Alistair. With all passengers safely aboard, the jet engines boomed on. Thomas reclined the seat into a sleep position and stared out the window as the plane taxied to the runway.

I hate being rude to Alistair, but I don't want to discuss this now. Not when we're about to take an eight-hour flight to Toronto. Alistair would talk the whole eight hours, telling me everything I did wrong, and I'd end up with a headache on top of my heartbreak.

It's times like these where the drugs hid my pain, but now that I've put drugs behind me, what can I do?

I remember our early days, when we played small clubs and venues, made a CD and tried to distribute it without a record deal. Our CD never made the money we expected, but then our manager called one day and said we had an opportunity to open for a major artist in a handful of cities. The lead singer of his original opening band was arrested the night before and they were desperate for a replacement. Naturally we jumped at the chance.

Looking out from backstage, I saw how large the audience was; we'd never played for a crowd of that size before. That's when it hit me that we were an unknown act opening for a well-known artist. Our band would be heckled, or people would yell for the bigger artist to come out. Thinking of all that gave me a massive anxiety attack as our stage appearance neared. Our manager, Andy, knew the look well and separated me from the other member. He led me to the back room where he pulled out a bag of small pills. I still remember him saying, "Next time I'll have something stronger." I knew he meant hard drugs, but thought, "I would never do that." I swallowed the pills and performed on stage. It took the edge off, but didn't completely remove my anxiety. Our popularity grew tremendously after that tour, and I relied on those small pills for every performance. Eventually, Andy taught me how to sniff cocaine; that was the worst mistake of my life.

Money poured in, Access was hot, and so was my addiction. I didn't need Andy as the middleman anymore; backstage crew members made purchases for me. My drug tolerance increased, and I used them everywhere and every day.

Access received a lucrative recording contract. We purchased fancy cars and homes. I paid off the loan on my mother's shop, bought her and Gran their own homes in great neighborhoods. When my big brother got engaged, I bought his house as a wedding gift. My whole family was proud of me; it felt really good to have them look at me with approval.

At first, my family didn't notice anything wrong; though later, my brother, James, became suspicious of my high energy and frequent bathroom breaks. He decided to bust in on me one time, and caught me in the act of snorting. That was all it took. "What the hell are you doing?" he shouted. I was angry with him for busting in on my privacy, and our heated argument was heard throughout the house. When my grandmother came and found out what we were fighting about, she joined James and sided against me. They both wanted to know why I was ruining my life by doing drugs. "It's not a big deal, everyone in the industry does drugs," was my reply.

From that day, James watched my every move. As the older brother, he was used to watching out for me; but we were no longer children, and I didn't appreciate the concern. I told him I was a grown man who could do whatever I wanted to do. My life wasn't his business.

James and Gran never let up on my drug habit; the confrontations and arguments were tiring. Neither had any idea of the stress and pressure I dealt with each time I stepped on stage; they couldn't relate. I moved from the family home and bought myself a large place in Richmond. There, I could party with my friends whenever I wanted without having to argue about it. My mum would visit sometimes, but I'd stopped taking calls from my brother and grandmother. Looking back, I realize I was just ignorant. They cared about me; they were the only ones who did.

Judy came into my life when she replaced one of our backup singers. She was gorgeous eye candy and she knew it—long blonde hair, gorgeous lips, delicious curves, all of her outfits stretched over her body in just the right way.

I make an effort to not get involved with staff because things can get messy and unprofessional; but it was impossible to keep that rule with Judy around. One of our backstage crew members was also my regular supplier, turns out he was Judy's supplier too. Once we discovered our shared interest, she became my snorting buddy. Sometimes I sent her to make a buy for me, then we'd snort together in my hotel room. Cocaine and sex went well together. Quickly, it seemed logical for Judy to move in with me, and we lived together for more than three years. Despite our addictions, she was my partner in every way and I loved her.

After making love one night, I asked her to marry me and she said yes. My mum was the one who helped me with personal things so I asked her to help Judy plan the wedding. My manager thought marrying Judy was a bad idea—he thought our record sales would drop once I was married. But I knew the only thing he was worried about was less money in his pocket since he received a percentage of our sales, so I wasn't about to take advice from him.

I introduced Judy as my fiancée to James and his wife, Sarah, and they didn't say much. Truth be told, it was an awkward situation since I hardly spoke to them anymore. Gran was never at home when I tried to introduce her to Judy, but James and Sarah said they didn't know where she was. Mick and Alistair didn't show any excitement about my engagement either. I expected more from Alistair since he was my best friend—and was to be the best man— but I knew Alistair didn't like the fact that Judy and I occasionally got high. I had hoped he would overlook that and give me some pointers or something, but that's not how things turned out.

We were finishing up a tour and I wanted the wedding to take place after that. Mom and Judy were checking out venues for the wedding and organizing all the other things that come with that kind of event. Then, one day, out of the blue, Judy called to say she no longer wanted to marry me. She'd already packed and left the house before I came home. She just walked out of my life and out of the band. It was the coldest thing anyone had done to me. She never gave me a reason for why she changed her mind, and I haven't seen or heard from her since that day. My mum told me I was better off, she thought Judy was just a gold digger anyway, but her statement upset me; Judy was my woman and I never saw her as a gold digger.

My addiction spiraled after Judy left; I stayed high all of the time, and the frequent usage started to affect my voice. I also started getting these embarrassing nose bleeds from the sores in my nose, and I never stopped sniffing because the post-nasal drip in my throat was continuous. Alistair said my addition was out of hand; his arguing was worse than with James. Of course, I didn't want to hear it. Then one evening I snorted as usual, but along with the high came throbbing chest pains. Someone called an ambulance and I was rushed to the hospital; luckily it wasn't a heart attack, but suddenly the public knew all about my addiction. Turns out, the photographer I'd punched, Lemmings, made it his mission to take photos of me whenever he could. He found out I was in the hospital, and the next morning the papers were all writing about how I almost overdosed on cocaine. Lemmings had gotten pictures of me when I was leaving the hospital, looking very rough. Even I had a hard time seeing those pictures in the papers.

My grandmother surprised me with a visit the next day. She showed up with a cane, bullied her way into my home, and proceeded to tell me off. It'd been such a long time since I'd seen her, and her weight had gone down. What I didn't know was that she'd had a stroke six months before. Gran told the family to not let me know because she didn't want me coming to her hospital room stoned; said she couldn't take seeing me like that anymore. I felt like crap knowing that Gran was ashamed of what I had become; that hurt more than anything. As she yelled at me, she started crying, and seeing her cry both broke my heart and opened my eyes. I could finally see that I was killing myself, and hurting my family, with my addiction.

Gran stayed with me that day, cleaning me up and making me dinner. When she implored me to go to rehab, I relented. My current batch of friends who hung out with me for free drugs weren't happy to hear that, but Gran got up and kicked them all out the house, using her cane on the stubborn ones.

Rehab was a four-month program; the first month was dreadful. I couldn't sleep and my cravings drove me insane. I had to forced myself to learn new lifestyle choices along with healthier ways to deal with my anxiety. Gran called me every week to see how I was doing. She had faith in me even though my mother and brother had given up. Gran would always say she was praying for me. Sounds silly, but I believe that made a difference in my recovery; knowing that someone I loved was rooting for me gave me extra strength to fight my addiction. When the program was completed, I joined a sobriety group and started socializing again. Avoiding all of my previous drug friends was tough, but I couldn't allow myself to get pulled back into that world.

I'd never thought dating would be an issue for me, but I was a different person after rehab. In the past, cocaine gave me confidence and made all the women appear sexier. I've had a few random dates since my recovery, but none made me want to build a relationship. I haven't had a serious relationship since Judy left me. Years have gone by, and I was beginning to think something was wrong with me, or that the drugs had damaged me somehow in that area. But on that one rainy night when I looked into that car and saw the face of the woman I'd been listening too, I felt something; and I wanted to feel it again. I gave her my cell number and was racking my brain, wondering how to call her for a date. When I saw the photo of her car pasted all over the tabloid, I felt bad and planned to call to apologize; but I was also happy to use the opportunity to see her again. The lunch was wonderful, we talked for hours, though I never noticed the time; we connected like old friends. That wasn't supposed to be a date, but it ended as one for me. I decided to pursue her the only way I knew how; but, unlike other women who've been in my life, Simone wasn't so enamored with my presence that she was willing to do whatever I liked. Dating her was hard work.

Sleeping with Simone was the best and worst thing I ever did. It made her break up with me; yet, making love solidified a bond between us I've never shared with any woman. This breakup is emotional hell; I can't stop thinking about her or the night we had. The memories torture me, they remind me of what I can never have again.

"Thom! Are you sleeping with your eyes open? Come on man, we've landed; get off the plane," shouted Alistair. Bewildered, Thomas jumped out of his sleep state and peered out the small jet window, where sheets of dry snow blew across the airstrip. The stark, cold landscape appeared uninhabited. All the band members grimaced when the frigid Canadian air slapped their faces as they exited the jet. Only Thomas welcomed the sting on his cheeks. He welcomed anything that took his mind off Simone.

"Thom, have you seen this?" Alistair yelled. He showed Thomas his phone. "Cynthia took a picture of a newspaper showing a picture of Simone leaving your home Saturday morning."

This is the last thing either of us needed, thought Thomas. "Lemmings has gotten out of hand; he needs to get a life. Somehow, I have to apologize to her," said Thomas.

"What do you mean, somehow? You guys had a little spat, right? Just call her," suggested Alistair.

Thomas sighed. "She doesn't want to hear from me, she broke it off."

"What? What happened? What did you do? Cynthia was just saying how you two look good together."

"What makes you think I did anything wrong? She stayed behind after the dinner to help me clean up, we had some wine to relax...then we made love. She woke up and realize she broke one of her 'Christian rules'"—Thomas threw up air quotes as he muttered the term—"so she told me she doesn't want to see me again."

"Wait, you made love? Isn't she one of those strict Christians? Man, how could you do that?" asked Alistair.

"Are you seriously asking me that question? How could I not? You know how I feel about her," said Thomas.

"So let me see if I understand correctly. You waited until she was tired, then you plied her with wine, and pounced on her?"

"No, no, it wasn't like that at all. Yes, I gave her a couple glasses of wine—she loves that wine by the way. She was tired so I gave her a foot massage." Alistair made a face at him. "OK, yes, I made advances, I am a man after all, but I didn't pounce on her. We both enjoyed the evening more than we had planned. My theory is she felt guilty for having sex and now she's punishing both of us by ending it. That's the only way to guarantee it doesn't happen again."

"Are you agreeing to this? I mean, what do you want?" asked Alistair.

"You speak as if I have a choice in the matter. Obviously I don't want to give her up, but what can I do? How can I convince her to put her faith aside and be with me again?" Thomas's phone started ringing before Alistair could answer. Thomas answered: "Hi Gran, how are you?"

"I'm fine sweetheart, how are you? I'm looking at the papers this morning, and I see you have a new girlfriend, she's pretty. According to the Daily View, it's serious. Why haven't you mentioned her to me or your mother?"

"Gran slow down, we haven't been dating long. I only met her a couple months ago."

"Wait Thom, your mother wants to speak with you."

Exasperated, Thomas closed his eyes before replying, "Hi Mum."

"Thom, when are you going to leave those gold diggers alone?" asked his mother.

"Mum, she's not a gold digger, she didn't spend time with me for money."

"Thom, you can be so naïve, have you forgotten Judy?"

"Mum, please don't go there, that's in my past. Look, I have to go, they need me; I'll call you later, OK? Goodbye."

Alistair snickered, "There's nobody calling you. Hey, why doesn't your mother like anyone you date? Did she give your brother a hard time, too?"

"Actually, now that I think of it, no; she didn't seem bothered when he started dating Sarah."

"Maybe she really likes her daughter-in-law. How is James doing anyway?"

"He's doing well; Sarah just had their third and final child. She said she's fed up with having cesareans, because, and I quote, 'the Lloyds have such big-headed babies they can't be born the normal way.' How about your kids? How old are Amy and Garth, they must be getting up in age?"

"Well, Amy is twelve now and Garth is five," said Alistair.

"Wow, time is going by fast; before you know it Amy will be at the university."

"Thankfully that's some ways off. Once they go to university, that's it, they start their own lives. I want to enjoy them as much as possible while they're still with me."

****

It's been a tough three weeks of the tour so far. I caught a cold in Toronto that was in full phlegm effect by the time we arrived in Boston for the US tour. I pumped myself full of antioxidants and cold medicines in the hotel room while Alistair and the rest of the band went out on the town. By the time we flew back to England for the Christmas break week I was in excellent health, physically, but Simone still remained on my mind. The only songs I was able to write during the flights were love ballads; this has to stop.

By the time Access's plane touched down at Luton Airport, Thomas had gotten his emotions in check; he changed his demeanor, pulling himself together so that his family wouldn't pick up on his misery. The family was having Christmas at James's house, and Thomas looked forward to seeing his niece and nephews again—they changed so much every time he visited—but his mind kept drifting to Simone so he decided to send her a text.

"Hey, Simone, I was just thinking about you. I want to wish you and your family a Merry Christmas. Love, Thomas."

"Uncle Thom's here, Uncle Thom's here!" Thomas's four-year-old nephew, Colin, screamed his arrival after he opened the door.

Thomas picked him up. "What are you doing opening the door all by yourself? I could have been a monster," he said.

"You're no monster," replied Colin. Thomas gave Colin a hug before placing his nephew on his shoulders; then he rolled his suitcases into the foyer and closed the door.

"Colin, what did I tell you about opening the door?" said

Sarah as she came and gave Thomas a hug. "It's good to see you, Thom, come in."

James, who now carried an ample paunch, came down the stairs to the foyer area and said, "It's about time you showed up. What took you so long?"

"Well, I could have arrived sooner if my loving brother had bothered to pick me up from the airport," replied Thomas.

"As long as there are taxis, that day will never come," said James.

"Sarah, why do you put up with this ogre?" Thomas joked. "OK, where am I sleeping today?"

"You're taking my room, Mom's making me sleep in Jennifer's room," said Colin.

"Where is your big sister anyway?"

"She's in the kitchen with Nana and Grandma," said Colin.

Thomas walked towards the kitchen as he called over his shoulder, "Be a dear and put away my bags, James old boy."

James rolled his eyes and said, "Listen you, this isn't the Ritz Carlton, pick up your own bags."

"Hi, sweetheart," Thomas's mother said as she kissed him. "You've been here less than two minutes and you're already teasing your brother."

"I enjoy teasing him, it's one of the few pleasures in my life," said Thomas.

James overheard the exchange and said, "Oh, I'm pretty sure you've been having some other pleasures lately. What did you do to the poor girl to make her leave you so early in the morning?" James teased. He waited for a witty comeback but Thomas made no reply. Instead, he kissed and greeted his fifteen-year-old niece, Jennifer, before giving his grandmother a warm hug.

Later in the day, Thomas and James watched a football match together. James knew his brother's character well. He could tell that Thomas was depressed, though he tried to hide it. When the game came to a break, James asked, "So, who is this woman you're seeing? Is it serious?"

Thomas replied, "No, not anymore, and I don't want to talk about it."

James sighed. He was used to his brother shutting him out of his life, but he always kept a watchful eye over him to make sure Thomas didn't relapse. He never wanted to see his little brother like that again.

CHAPTER TWELVE
CHRISTMAS

Sunday morning, Simone prepared to attend church services. As she did, her doorbell rang, though she wasn't expecting anyone. When she saw that it was only Derrick, Simone opened the door in her robe. Her friend was looking down his nose at her. "Hi Derrick, I wasn't expecting a visit from you this morning. What's up?" she asked.

"Maybe you should tell me. You ought to have a look at this," he said as he handed her one of the English gossip newspapers. On the second page was a huge photo of Simone with the headline: "*Tom's mysterious gal pal exits home in wee morning hours.*" Simone was in shock; she couldn't believe someone had taken a photo of her. Now all of England knew she'd slept with Thomas Lloyd. *Could this get any worse?* she wondered. As she looked up, Derrick turned and walked out the door, slamming it closed.

Simone didn't need to tell Nikki about the newspaper; Derrick took care of that. During the week, Simone received flowers from Thomas; he'd heard about the newspaper article and wanted to apologize for it. Doing business as usual was difficult, she saw a few of Derrick's other tenants peer through the window at her, and Simone had no doubt their sudden interest in her shop had to do with Derrick spreading the word about her affair. She even took Thomas's portrait down, hoping her customers wouldn't make the connection.

****

The days passed quickly, and it was quickly time for Simone to spend time with her family. She'd closed the shop and was preparing to leave for New York the next day. After she packed the gifts she'd bought for her family and friends, she was walking through her shop, looking for anything she may have forgotten to pack, when she noticed a white envelope under the door. *That's odd*, she thought. She opened it and saw that it was from Derrick.

> *Hi Simone, I didn't want to disturb you while you worked but I wanted you to have this note before you left for the holiday. As you know, the terms of the lease state that your rate could increase after fifteen months, the date of which will be March 1ST. I just wanted to give you a heads up because I will be raising the rent by 5 percent to cover costs.*
>
> *Please enjoy your holidays.*
>
> *Sincerely,*
> *Derrick*

The next morning, Simone checked her studio, making certain everything was turned off. Her bags were packed, and Nikki had called to let her know that she was waiting in the car outside to drop her at the airport. Simone walked out with her luggage and was locking the door behind her when someone called her name. As she turned around, she saw a camera lens a few yards from her face, the photographer snapping away, taking pictures of her every movement. She was caught off guard for a few seconds before realizing that the man must be Thomas's rogue photographer who'd somehow discovered where she lived. She walked quickly with her suitcase to Nikki's waiting car.

"Simone are you alright?" Nikki asked. "I saw that idiot; he must have taken a thousand pictures already, I don't know why he's still standing there."

"Maybe he's waiting for Thomas to walk out my door. Well, at least I won't be here to see tomorrow's papers. And please tell your cousin Derrick to hold all newspaper deliveries from now on."

"Simone, forget Derrick, I don't know what's gotten into him. He's acting like an idiot. I'm sorry I ever talked you into renting from him."

"It's fine Nikki, I can handle Derrick. I'm more concerned with this photographer potentially scaring off my customers."

"Maybe you should call Thomas, he might be able to help," suggested Nikki.

"I can't, I'm trying to put that relationship behind me. Besides, it's not his fault. If I didn't stay the night, this would not be happening. I made a bad decision and I'm paying for it."

****

After a delayed connecting flight in Ireland, Simone's plane landed at JFK airport in the late afternoon. The airport was packed with holiday travelers, and it took her over an hour to get a taxi.

New York's air was frigid with ice and snow already stuck to the ground, but Simone didn't mind; she was so happy to be back she felt like kissing the dirty snow. All her headaches were left behind in England, and she looked forward to spending time with Martin and her mother. The taxi pulled up to the three-story row home in Cobble Hill, Brooklyn, and Simone paid the driver before pulling her luggage up the tall flight of stairs to the front door.

When she entered the foyer, Simone was greeted with the sweet smell of the live Christmas tree that sat in front of the living room bay window. Laura had decorated every corner of the living/dining room area. Two mini live Christmas trees were arranged on the dining room buffet, which was also covered with the same warm white lights as the living room tree. All three trees were loaded with ornaments the family had collected through the years, and the presents under the tree bore colorful hand-tied ribbons and metallic-glittered giftwrap.

Simone walked towards the voices coming from the kitchen. "Look who just crawled in. You were supposed to be here a few hours ago," said Martin.

"Well hello to you too, my gosh you are always so rude," she said jokingly as she walked over to hug her brother. "Hi Mom," she gave her mother a long hug, "I missed you so much."

"Sweetheart, I missed you too."

"Yeah Simone, maybe you should come home more often," hinted Martin.

"Listen smart-aleck, I'm running a new business, and it needs to be nurtured by its sole employee, so I have to be there as much as possible. Where's Carly?"

"Ah, Carly decided to spend the holidays with her parents this year," Martin said solemnly.

"Oh, I'm so sorry to hear that; she usually keeps you in check. When are you two coming back for a visit?" she asked him.

"Well if I come, you'd better take time off to spend with me, I'm not coming just to watch you work all day," quipped Martin.

"Martin, stop picking on your sister, she just came home; let her relax first," said her mother.

"Yes Martin, stop picking on me, my bags are in the living room by the way." Martin grumbled on his way to the living room.

"So, Simi, now that Martin's gone, tell me about your 'friend.'"

"Oh Mom, it's nothing. We went on a few dates, but our lifestyles are too different for our relationship to work, so I broke it off."

"Simone, I know you don't like me saying this, but you are getting older and I know you always wanted a family..."

"Mom, I'm still in my twenties, and are we really going to have this conversation? I thought you wanted me to rest," said Simone.

"You're right, I'll leave it alone for now; let's talk about something else. Are you going to bake anything tomorrow?"

"Yes, but I haven't made up my mind yet about what to make." Simone continued to discuss baking with her mother because she was so happy to change the subject. She hated keeping secrets from to her mom, but she wasn't ready to talk about Thomas yet, especially since she was missing him so much.

****

Simone awoke late in the morning at 11 AM. Oversleeping was out of character for her, but she believed her body clock was adjusting to jet lag. When she did go downstairs, her mother and brother were settled in the living room watching the news.

"Good morning Simone, I left your breakfast in the oven," said Laura.

"Thanks, Mom. Martin, did you leave any coffee for me?"

"Don't you Brits drink tea?" he teased.

"That's so cliché, lots of Brits drink coffee and there are tons of coffee shops throughout London."

Martin nudged his mother. "You heard that Mom, she considers herself a Brit now," he teased again.

Their mother took the newspaper out of Martin's hand, rolled it up, and smacked him on the head with it before returning the paper to him. "I told you to leave your sister alone." Simone laughed as she walked into the kitchen. She poured coffee into a large mug, then tossed a sweetener and some milk into it; but when she sipped the coffee it tasted awful.

She spit it back in the cup and yelled to the living room, "Martin, did you make the coffee?"

"Honey I made the coffee, is everything OK?" asked Laura.

"It's fine Mom," Simone said as she poured the drink into the sink. She grabbed the plate of home fries and spinach quiche her mom had left for her in the oven. Normally she'd have ketchup on her home fries, but for some reason that combination was turning her off today. After finishing her breakfast, Simone sat in the living room with Martin and her mother.

"What are you making for Christmas dinner, Mom?" she asked.

"I'm going to make a spiral ham, a rack of lamb, and a turkey for you with all the trimmings since you didn't have Thanksgiving."

"Oh, you don't have to cook turkey for me, one of my friends threw a nice Thanksgiving dinner for me on the Friday after, there was even pumpkin pie," said Simone.

"Simone, that was a very nice thing for them to do, which friend was this?" asked Laura.

"Thomas."

"Oh, Thomas again," said her mother.

"Who's Thomas?" asked Martin.

"He's Simi's new friend who she doesn't want to talk about."

Martin squinted over his newspaper at Simone and asked, "What kind of friend is this, you never told me you had a boyfriend."

Simone sighed. "We're just friends, he wanted to do something nice for me when he realized I wasn't coming home for Thanksgiving. Look, I have to go to the supermarket to buy some things before I start baking," said Simone.

"Honey I can do that for you, why don't you just rest," said Laura.

"That's alright Mom, I'm well rested. Besides, I want to look around the neighborhood. I'll be back soon."

Martin yelled out, "Remember to use bills that don't have the Queen's face on them," he teased.

"Your jokes are so lame Martin," Simone said before leaving. Simone loved her red-haired brother despite the teasing. She wished they lived closer, but even if she'd stayed in New York, he would still be far. After graduation from college, Martin had taken a good job offer in Washington, DC, and had lived there ever since.

The weather was much better today. The sun was shining, melting some of the snow and ice. Simone headed towards the avenue where the supermarket was but veered down a different street to a new coffee shop she'd spotted. Inside, she ordered her coffee and sat at the back of the shop looking out the window. She noticed several unread text messages on her phone. She answered one from Nikki, wishing her a Merry Christmas with her family. There was one from Becky asking where she'd been the past two Sundays. Simone quickly sent an apology and told Becky that she would explain everything when she returned home after the holidays; she wished Becky a Merry Christmas too. Thinking of Becky, Simone realized that the Bible study leader could have helped advise her about her dating situation before it became disastrous; maybe then the outcome would have been different. In any case, Simone realized she needed to speak to someone who understood her position; so she texted her high school friend Marcy.

"Hmm." The coffee smelled great, but Simone grimaced; it made her stomach cramp when it went down. She threw it out and ordered a cup of tea to go. She had no problems drinking the tea on the way to the supermarket.

The first floor of the family home was empty when Simone returned from the store. She placed all of the ingredients needed for the desserts she planned to make on the kitchen counter. Her plan was to make a chocolate Yule log (a favorite of hers that her grandmother used to make), spritz cookies, and a layered spice cake with cream cheese frosting.

The last tray of cookies was cooling just before dinner time. Simone cleaned the kitchen and decided to take a little nap because her body clock was still adjusting to the time difference. The next day her aunt, uncle, and cousins would come over, and she'd help her mother prepare the food. Martin would do nothing as usual, she reasoned, but it was still nice to have him around. This was how they always spent Christmas after her parents' divorce.

Though they had new traditions now, the perfect Christmas's had been spent with their father; Simone reminisced about when her dad would spontaneously sing Christmas songs (he had a wonderful voice), and complained that the house was too quiet for the holiday. Though she smiled at the memories, the current silence brought her back to the present, where her smile faded before her eyes closed.

Simone awoke at 5 AM and couldn't sleep anymore. She

saw several messages when she looked at her phone. Thomas had wished her and her family a Merry Christmas; he'd sent her the cutest picture of himself with two kids by his side; she figured they must be his niece and nephew. Seeing his photo brought up those feelings she was trying to dismiss. Simone replied back, *"I love the picture. I hope you and your family have a wonderful Christmas too."*

After getting dressed, she went downstairs to prepare Christmas breakfast for her mom and Martin. She made multigrain waffles, Canadian bacon, poached eggs, and a mixed berry smoothie.

The three family members ate their breakfast and opened presents in relative silence, then Simone and Laura went to the kitchen to prepare Christmas dinner. Martin's only responsibility was to set the table; Laura asked him to add one more placement, but didn't say for whom.

While Simone and her mother prepared the dishes, Martin put his feet up and watched a few football games. He was still angry with his girlfriend, Carly, for not coming to his mother's for Christmas, but he missed not being with her during the holiday, so he decided to call.

Martin and Carly became a couple while attending college; they had been living together in an apartment for the past five years. Martin enjoyed their life the way it was, but Carly was ready for change. She kept bringing up the possibilities of children and buying a permanent home; Martin reassured her that he wanted the same things, someday, but not right then. He didn't understand the rush; they were only in their early thirties. Martin frowned at the phone, every call he'd made to her in the past two days had gone to voicemail.

"Martin! The doorbell is ringing, answer the door!" Laura screamed. The screaming made Martin jump, accidently hanging up his fifth call to Carly today. He scrambled to the door to cease the succession of knocking and bell ringing.

"Hey, Martin, what took you so long to open the door? It's freezing out here!" said his uncle.

"Merry Christmas, Uncle Vic, Aunt Annie." His twin cousins, ten-year-olds Raymond and Richard, came in behind their parents. The boys barely nodded acknowledgement, both so engrossed with their phones. Uncle Victor, Laura's little brother, grew up in the family home with their Armenian and Irish parents.

Simone and Laura exited the kitchen to kiss and greet everyone. Laura had already set up platters of hors d'oeuvres, along with Simone's baked cookies and biscotti, in the dining room.

Their Christmas dinner table spread was perfectly arranged using Laura's family antique stemware. All family members were on their way to their seats when the doorbell rang again. Martin was already at the door when Simone looked up to see their unknown guest—much to her surprise, it was her father who stepped through the doorway. Simone smiled but held her breath, waiting for Cindy to follow him through the doorway. When her dad closed the door behind himself, no Cindy in sight, she exhaled a sigh of relief. Simone eyed Martin for an explanation, but her brother only shrugged his shoulders. He was just as confused as Simone. Their mother, on the other hand, was very nonchalant about it, which indicated to Simone that Laura had known he was coming. Simone gave her father a hug, then announced to everyone that dinner was ready. The family stood around the table while Simone said grace. She enjoyed having her parents and family together, collectively eating a meal peacefully. It was the best Christmas gift she'd received.

When dinner was over, the family sat around talking and

laughing. Simone sat beside her father, intending to pick his brain to find out where Cindy was, but he looked worn out and it was Christmas, so she left it for later.

The next morning Simone was up early again; hungry and slightly nauseous at the same time. She got dressed and went downstairs to raid the refrigerator. She loved holiday meal leftovers, and she'd just plated ham, mac and cheese, baked sweet potatoes, and sautéed spinach when Martin interrupted her early morning feast.

"Goodness Simone, you're pigging out."

She looked down at her plate and said, "It does look like a lot of food doesn't it?"

"Did you make any coffee?" asked Martin.

"Good morning to you too," she said sarcastically. "No, I didn't make any coffee."

"You could have at least made some for Dad," said Martin.

"Wait, Dad is still here?" she whispered. "What's going on?"

"I have no idea; thought I was the only one out of the loop. Did you know he was coming?"

"No, I was just as shocked as you were. Where is he sleeping?" she asked.

"In my room of course. I didn't know he was staying over. He just said, 'You mind if I bunk with you? Your mother said I could stay overnight.'"

"Did you ask him about Cindy?" asked Simone.

"Didn't anyone tell you that Cindy left him?"

"No, Mom didn't tell me and neither did you. When did that happen?"

"I thought you already knew. They've been apart for a few months now; he didn't want to talk about it too much."

"Do you know why they broke up?" she asked.

Just then their father walked in and said, "I can tell you why we broke up if you want to hear it from me."

"Sorry Dad, we didn't know you were up," said Simone.

"Don't worry about it, I have to tell you two something anyway; I didn't want to spoil Christmas day," he replied, "but I have prostate cancer. I was diagnosed this summer and I'm getting treatment for it. I've opted to have a few sessions of external beam radiation. Cindy couldn't handle the news, so she left me when I told her about it."

"Dad, I'm so sorry, why didn't you tell us?" asked Simone.

"I didn't want to worry anyone; I know you have your own lives. Besides, they caught it early and the outcome looks promising," said her father.

Simone hugged her father and said, "Dad, don't worry about stressing us out, we're adults. There's no need to protect us anymore; promise us that you will keep us up to date with your progress."

Simone and Martin spent the rest of the day with their father before he left to fly back to Florida.

The next day, Simone planned a visit to her friend. The subway ride was short, but the jerking movement of the train made her nauseous to the point where her stomach churned when she left the train. Though she exited the subway and was walking in fresh air, the nausea didn't go away. She soon reached Marcy's house, but when Marcy opened the door, Simone had no time for greetings; she quickly asked for the bathroom. Once inside, Simone vomited all the contents of her stomach.

Marcy called out, "Simone, are you alright?"

Simone felt awful. She cleaned up and walked out of the bathroom. "Sorry Marcy, I don't know why but my stomach is acting up, and the subway ride made it worse."

"Maybe it's just you getting used to the New York subway

smells again. You've lived away so long that you're no longer immune to it."

Marcy's mother walked down the hall to see what had happened. "Simone, it's so nice to see you." She came over and gave Simone a hug. Then she stepped back and squinted, looking at Simone again.

"What's wrong, Mrs. Gabiner, why are you looking at me like that?"

"Simone, are you pregnant?" asked Mrs. Gabiner.

"What? No, I can't be, I just have an upset stomach. It's been sensitive since I arrived back in New York," said Simone.

"Hmmm, I don't know why, but…I just have that feeling," said Mrs. Gabiner.

"Mom, your early pregnancy vibes are off this time; you know Simone isn't like that," said Marcy.

Although Simone kept calm on the outside, fear crept in on the inside; but then she dismissed the notion of her being pregnant because she'd had sex only once recently.

Simone and Marcy reminisced about their old high school days before both went away to college. Marcy studied finance, and she met her husband while working at a firm on Wall Street. The two married three years ago with Simone as the maid of honor. Marcy was the first of her friends to have a child, and this was the first time Simone had held Marcy's nine-month-old baby girl.

Simone's visit lasted several hours. On her way home, Mrs. Gabiner's question stayed on her mind. She wanted to rule out a pregnancy as the source of her queasiness, and she found herself searching the aisles of the neighborhood drugstore before going home. Thankfully, Laura and Martin were watching a movie when she arrived. Simone told them she was going to bed early because she was tired.

Once inside the bathroom, she pulled the box from the

small bag. The instructions were simple. Simone opened the test, peed on the stick, and waited with her head in her hands. When the allotted time passed, she looked at the test stick. It showed two wide pink stipes, *Positive!* "No!" she whispered to no one in the bathroom. Sitting on the edge of the tub with her head in her hands, Simone inwardly berated herself for sleeping with Thomas. Then she thought that the test may be flawed. Simone planned to make a doctor's appointment when she returned to London to confirm the test results.

The next morning she again awoke early. She immediately picked up her phone and texted Thomas.

"Good morning Thomas, please call me, I need to talk to you. It's important."

Later in the day over in London, Thomas was in his brother's backyard playing with his niece and nephew. He checked his phone and was happy to see Simone's text. Thomas's finger was poised to call Simone as she'd requested, but he stopped himself and thought, *"She wanted me to leave her alone so that's what I'm going to do."*

****

Laura and Simone had said their goodbyes to Martin when he left for home the day before. Knowing that Simone would also leave in three days, Laura was adamant about spending as much time as possible with her daughter. Simone, on the other hand, found herself keeping secrets from her mother again. She avoided eating breakfast with her mom because she discovered that her nausea was strongest in the morning. Dry toast and tea was the only meal she could tolerate after she woke. Lunch and dinner were easier to keep down, and Simone was learning to avoid certain foods that her stomach no longer tolerated.

It troubled her that two days had passed with no return text or call from Thomas. She thought about calling him, but she wanted to see a doctor first to confirm the pregnancy.

CHAPTER THIRTEEN
THE PRESENT

When she left England, Simone was glad to get away from her problems. But now she was glad to be back home. Before settling and unpacking, she called her doctor and made an appointment for the next day. Simone's next call was to Nikki, who confirmed that her name and picture had been in the paper after she'd left for New York, but Nikki didn't believe her customers would remember the article since it was old news now.

"On the bright side, since Thomas is out of town on tour, there's no reason for the creepy photographer to hang around," Nikki tried to reassure her friend.

"Nikki, I have a more serious problem to deal with." Simone filled Nikki in on all that had happened during her Christmas week.

"Oh Simone, I don't know what to say, that's terrible. I'm coming with you to the appointment."

"Thanks Nikki, it would be great if you could. I need someone with me right now."

Simone had trouble sleeping that night. She got out of bed and kneeled in prayer. She repeated her request for God to forgive her sin, a prayer she'd repeated numerous times since sleeping with Thomas. This time, she asked for help to get her through whatever news came to her tomorrow. Simone then returned to bed, where, just before she dozed off, Becky came to mind.

The shop wasn't busy in the morning; and thankfully only one customer mentioned seeing her in the tabloid. Simone's afternoon doctor's appointment couldn't come fast enough for her. She left as soon as possible, planning to get there early to meet up with Nikki. As Simone waited in the doctor's office, she thought of Thomas and wished he was there with her, but she reprimanded herself for wanting him. She reasoned she couldn't be with Thomas; she was going through this because of him and her weakness for him.

Nikki was running late, so when the nurse called for Simone, she went in alone. Simone had been a patient of the same gynecologist her entire time living in England, so the doctor knew Simone's history as a celibate patient. It was an embarrassing experience for her to tell the doctor why she was there. The medical provider tested for pregnancy and several STIs. Noticing her awkwardness about the additional tests, Doctor Rodsmith assured Simone that STI testing was routine with pregnancies.

"The pregnancy result will be available in five to ten minutes," said the nurse. Simone was told to go back to the waiting room and wait until they called her again; thankfully, when she got there, she found Nikki waiting.

Nikki gave her a big hug. "I'm sorry for being late, I couldn't find parking anywhere. What did they say?"

"That's alright Nikki, I'm waiting for the pregnancy results."

"How are you feeling? You seem so calm," asked Nikki.

"I'm trying to keep it together until I have an answer. Whatever happens, I'll take it one day at a time," said Simone.

"Miss Mills? the doctor is ready to see you," said the nurse.

Nikki came with Simone into the office. "Welcome back; I have all the results here. The STI tests are all negative, and congratulations; we confirmed that you are pregnant. The nurse will set up your sonogram appointment so that we can establish the age of the fetus, but based on your own calculations, you're probably about six weeks in. I'm here for you if you have any questions." So many thoughts were going through Simone's mind, but she said nothing, just thanked the doctor and left.

The two friends went to dinner afterwards to discuss the next step.

"Simone, what are you planning to do?" asked Nikki.

"I don't know. I was thinking of calling Thomas, but there's no reason to hurry. He can't do anything to change the circumstances."

"Simone, you have to tell him. What if he doesn't want a child?" said Nikki.

"At this point, the decision is not up to him. The baby is here whether he wants to have a life with it or not. I never planned to be a single mother, I'm sure most single mothers didn't plan to raise a child on their own, but they do what they have to."

"What about your business; can you cope with running a new business and caring for a baby?"

"I'm not sure of how I'm going to do it, but I'll have to try my best."

Later that night Simone called Becky and arranged to meet up after church on Sunday. She thought about telling her family, too; however, imagining how difficult the call would be and how upset her mother would become, she decided it wasn't the time to tell them.

Simone used to meet up with Becky after church regularly,

but those meetups had tapered off once Thomas entered the picture. Nevertheless, the two friends greeted each other with hugs as usual. Becky immediately sensed a great deal of anxiety in Simone, so she suggested they go to her home to have a private talk.

Once at Becky's house, Simone didn't know how to start the conversation; she had so much respect and admiration for Becky. After all, she was not just a long-time church member, she also sat on the church board. Becky often led Bible study, and the two had worked together on several ministry projects.

"Simone, what is wrong? You've been solemn throughout the service; it's not like you. I know you have something on your mind," said Becky.

Simone told her friend everything about her relationship with Thomas, her pregnancy, and her worries about how this would affect her future.

"Simone, you've already asked Christ to forgive your sin. That was the correct thing to do, but forgiveness doesn't mean the results of your sin are erased. After asking for forgiveness, you must allow Christ to carry your burden, which, in this case, includes the guilt you're carrying around. You have to give your problem to God to work on, but He can't help you with it if you refuse to forgive yourself for what you've done."

"Becky, you don't understand. Thomas didn't pressure me into having sex, I participated willingly. I gave in to my feelings. I knew it was wrong, but I did it anyway. How can I forgive myself?"

"Simone, we all sin and fall short of the glory of God. Yes, we strive to be Christlike, but we are not Him. We struggle with desires of the flesh every day. In our present world, the temptation to have sex is everywhere: on television, movies, magazines, music, art, the list goes on. You're certainly not the first to give into sexual temptation.

"Simone, you're fairly new to our church so I realize you've never heard my testimony. You know I have a son, but did you know that he is twenty years old?"

"Twenty?" gasped Simone, certain that her friend was in her early thirties.

"Yes, I gave birth when I was just fifteen. I came from a broken home—my father left our family when I was ten years old and he never looked back. There was no communication, no birthday cards, not even phone calls. After he left, my mother spent all her spare time on boyfriends; she was no longer concerned about me. It didn't matter if I stayed out all night, she wasn't waiting up for me to come home. I felt as though I'd lost both parents. I started looking to others for the love and attention I wasn't receiving at home. I hung out with the wrong crowd, started having sex very early. My friends drank alcohol, so I did it too; I thought everyone was doing it. I became pregnant at fourteen. One day, my mother noticed that my shirts were getting tight in my abdomen and she took me to the clinic. When they told us I was pregnant, she called me a little tramp and slapped me. Then she kicked me out. The social worker sent me to a home for unwed teen mothers. When people looked at me, they looked at my stomach; I could see the judgment in their eyes. It was a horrible time in my life.

"On Saturdays in the home, a ministry group would come and hold a service for us. It was through that service, which was sponsored by our church, that I was introduced to Christ. When I gave my life to Christ, I no longer felt like a hopeless mess, though I still struggled with rejection. Here I was, fifteen years old, my son without his father or any help from my family. The people from the ministry encouraged me to read the Word and to pray, and they would always pray with me.

"God spoke to my heart one day and made me realize that though He'd already forgiven me for what I'd done when I'd asked Him to, I never forgave myself. This was the burden I carried with me that blocked my blessings. So, I prayed and asked Jesus to help me forgive myself, and eventually I did.

"And here I am. I raised my son on my own, he's doing well in the military, and I'm happy with my life."

"Becky, I'm sorry I never knew your past or what you went through. You seem so confident and happy all the time. I've always wanted to be more like you."

"Simone, being a single parent was tough; and to this day, my mother still does not speak to me. If I hadn't committed to Christ, I would not be the person you see today. That said, I'm not perfect in my Christian walk; no one is. Realizing and admitting that you are not perfect is the only way to stay humble and keep yourself from being a hypocrite. 1 John 1:9 states that 'if we confess our sins, He is faithful and just to forgive us our sins, and to cleanse us from all unrighteousness.'

"You have asked for forgiveness of your sin, now you must believe that you are forgiven; it's time for you to forgive yourself. As for your future, take it one day at a time. Matthew 6:34 says, 'Do not worry about tomorrow, for tomorrow will worry about itself. Each day has enough trouble of its own.'"

"You're right Becky, I should stop worrying. It's easier said than done, but I have to find a way to let this guilt go."

"Simone, I'm here for you if you ever need someone to talk to or pray with, and don't ever feel ashamed to come to service. We are all sinners, and no one has the right or the power to condemn anyone who's repented of their sins."

****

Simone returned home that afternoon determined to get through to Thomas. Since he had ignored her texts, she decided to write him a letter, even though she wasn't certain when he was coming back from the tour. She had to tell him about the baby before she told anyone else.

Dear Thomas,

I hope your tour went well. I've called and sent you texts, but I did not hear back from you. Guess you're still upset with me.

If I didn't say it before, I'm sorry. I shouldn't have dated you or extended our relationship when I knew I had strong feelings for you. It was not my intention to hurt you or end our relationship so abruptly when I told you to leave. It's just that I was so disappointed in myself for losing control and doing something that I knew was wrong.

I know my lifestyle seems idiotic to you, and you're probably regretting the time we spent together, but something has resulted from the night we spent together. I found out that I'm pregnant. At this time I'm seven weeks along. It came as a shock to me since I know we used protection. In any case, I need to know if you want me to keep you informed about the pregnancy or if you want nothing to do with our child. Please get in touch with me.

Sincerely,
Simone

CHAPTER FOURTEEN
FAMILY

"The baby looks good and has a strong heartbeat," said the technician. Simone was amazed at how something so tiny had a heartbeat, but hearing it made her smile. She'd decided to go to her sonogram alone even though Nikki had offered to go. Simone wanted to get used to doing these things on her own; she knew she had a long road ahead as a single parent. She'd received no reply from Thomas, but figured he must still be on tour. This wasn't the type of information she wanted to send via voicemail or text; however, she felt it was important for Thomas to know as soon as possible, so she decided to give him another week before sending the information digitally.

At nine weeks pregnant, Simone was aware the pregnancy could start to show in another month. The nausea had become more frequent, and though Doctor Rodsmith had given her a list of foods to avoid, even when avoiding those foods, the nausea was still there.

When she arrived home from the ultrasound, she found a note tucked into her door.

I need to see you; can you come on Saturday at 10 AM? I'll send my driver.

Thomas.

Hmm, Thomas received my note but didn't call? That's not like him, maybe he's in shock, she thought.

The week flew by. Simone photographed a wedding and secured two new business clients. Brooklyn Graphics was doing well, which was great given that Derrick was increasing the rent.

That Saturday, Simone decided to bring the sonogram pictures of the baby. She hoped Thomas would want to see them. The driver *was* waiting for her outside, but this time it wasn't Thomas. The man drove her quietly to Thomas's house and escorted her out of the car to the front door. Libby opened the door; she said hello, but her cheerful demeanor was gone. As she took Simone's coat she whispered, "Brace yourself."

Bemused, Simone walked into the sitting room to find an older woman with a stern look sitting in a high-back chair at a desk.

"Hello dear, Thomas is not back from his tour, but he left me instructions for you," she said.

"I'm sorry, who are you?" asked Simone.

"Sorry, I don't mean to be rude. I'm Thomas's mother, we're very close. You haven't seen me before because I travel quite a bit. Now, let's discuss this issue. Please have a seat." Simone sat down in the small chair placed on the other side of the large desk.

Thomas's mother began. "I understand you're claiming to be pregnant with Thomas's child, and you intend on keeping the baby even though you and Thomas are no longer together. Can I ask why you want to keep the baby? Is it something you've always wanted?" asked Mrs. Lloyd.

"Actually, no, I had no intention of getting pregnant at this stage in my life. Can I ask what instructions you said you have for me?" Simone was becoming angry; she didn't like the fact that Thomas had set her up to speak with his mother instead of himself.

"Well, you Americans do like to get to the point. Alright then, I'll make this quick. Thomas has no interest in having children; he never has. He doesn't want to be in the child's life but he realizes he has some responsibility in the matter. That being said, we're prepared to offer you 200,000 pounds for you and your baby. There are conditions: you must carry out a paternity test to prove that the child is indeed Thomas's; you should be able to do that in a few weeks. Once we have a positive result, you will receive your money and everyone's happy."

Simone was so angry she was afraid to speak because she didn't know what would come out of her mouth. *How could this be Thomas's mother?* she thought. Simone got up, turned around, and left without replying. Libby handed over her coat. Simone could feel her blood pressure rising as she walked out of the house towards the car and motioned for the driver to open the door.

When the driver pulled up in front of her home, Simone saw the same photographer who had ambushed her before Christmas waiting on the pavement. Simone had had enough of this, so she walked briskly in the photographer's direction. Seeing her expression, Lemmings began to retreat.

"Why are you stalking me?" she yelled. The short man did not reply; the closer she came, the faster he ran away until he reached his car, got in, and pulled away.

Inside her studio, Simone was still in shock at what Thomas and his mother had planned. She'd never thought Thomas could be so cold.

Simone took a brief nap to calm herself down. When she awoke, the expectant mother was ready to straighten out the mess that was her life. Simone's first plan of action was dealing with Mark Lemmings; she had an idea of how to stop him from stalking her. Simone turned on her laptop and did some research. She started by looking up the pest photographer's background. *"OK, Mr. Lemmings, if you don't want to speak to me, I have to find someone you'll listen to,"* she said to herself. After purchasing a background search on Lemmings, she reviewed his personal contacts. The report listed the names and addresses of his employer, mother, wife, and his adult daughter who currently resided at a local university. Simone used her best stationery to write a letter to each individual. In each she introduced herself and explained the situation. Simone then politely pleaded with each of them to ask Lemmings to stop stalking her. She explained in the letter that his stalking was making her live in fear and causing her great distress. She implored each person she wrote to to ask him to let her live in peace. Simone prayed this would work because she had no other options.

Her next plan was to tell someone in her family about the pregnancy. Martin was her first choice; Simone didn't want to upset her father during his illness, and she knew her mother would automatically call her father if Simone relayed the information to her. *This is not going to be easy,* she thought.

"Hi Martin, are you busy?"

"Hey, no not very, just doing some tedious paperwork. So what's happening in London today? You don't usually call me when I'm at work. How's business?"

"Business is fine. I have some other things going on that I need to tell you about."

"Other things? This sounds serious sis, is something wrong...? Simone? Are you still there?"

"Martin, I'm pregnant."

"P-P-Pregnant? How did that happen! Wait a minute, don't tell me your new 'friend' is the father? Simone, how could you let

this happen? You've never once introduced any boyfriends to me or the family. A while back I thought maybe you weren't even into guys, and now you say you're pregnant?"

"Yes; my friend Thomas is the father. We were dating, and things...got out of hand."

"Where is he, what does he plan to do?"

"I haven't seen him yet, and I broke up with him before Christmas. He's out of the country for a few months. I did however, speak to his mother, and she offered me money to go away."

"What?! Who are these people you've gotten yourself mixed up with? Have you spoken to Mom?" asked Martin.

"No I haven't told Mom, and I don't want you speaking to Mom or Dad about this either. I don't want to stress out Dad while he's sick, and you know Mom will tell him everything," said Simone.

"Simi I'm sorry, I wish I could be there with you. I should come over and deal with this Thomas and his mother for how they've treated you."

"No Martin, it's OK, you don't have to come. I have everything under control; I'm seeing a doctor and so far everything is good."

"Simone, you may not want to hear this, but have you thought of getting rid of it?"

"You mean have an abortion? Why would I do that? It's not the baby's fault that I made a mistake."

"No, but mistakes can be corrected and your 'friend's mom' sounds like a real idiot. Think about it, do you want to have his baby? You have your business to worry about. Also, one day soon you'll have to tell Mom and Dad; they're going to ask about the father, too. They'll both be disappointed to hear he has no interest in the baby. Being a single parent is not easy; you have to think this through."

"Martin, I know the baby is not convenient. This couldn't have happened at a worse time; my business is picking up and there's no time to spare at this stage. But I can't get rid of my baby because I don't think it's the opportune time or because their father is an idiot."

"OK, OK, Simi, forget I said anything about that. Let me know if there's anything I can do. Maybe it's time for you to come back home, though. Your family's here, we can't help you from so far."

"Martin, I'd have to give up the business if I move back home."

"Listen, just think about it. In the meantime, I'll book a flight to see you soon."

"Alright Martin, it would be good to see you. Let me know later when you're thinking of coming."

"I will Simone, you take care of yourself and don't forget: you have to tell Mom."

Simone's next call was to Nikki; she filled her friend in on the meeting with Thomas's mother. Nikki refused to believe that Thomas would use his mother in that way, but she was faced with the fact that Thomas had never returned Simone's calls or texts.

CHAPTER FIFTEEN
THE PEST

The doorbell rang early in the morning while Simone was still in the rear of her apartment. She hurried to the door, believing the visitor was a customer, but when she opened it, she found Lemmings standing on the other side. This time he spoke.

"Good morning Ms. Mills, I need to speak to you about the letters." He seemed calm and composed, so Simone invited the man in and offered him a seat. "Ms. Mills, you sent a letter to my mother; she became very upset with me. Why did you do that? My mother is elderly and it's important that she doesn't get upset. My whole family is angry with me because of your letters."

"Mr. Lemmings, I apologize for upsetting your mother, but you forced my hand. I tried to talk to you, but you ran away; there was no other option. Look, I'm a photographer too. I understand that you take pictures of celebrities for a living, but there was no reason for you to camp outside my home. I'm not the celebrity, I'm just connected to a celebrity you hate. I understand that you and Thomas had a disagreement, but wasn't that years ago? And aren't you used to encountering angry celebrities in your line of work? I'm certain you don't go after everyone in the same manner. When you stalked me, you crossed over the line of professionalism into harassment. Something had to be done!"

"Alright, alright miss, I don't want to upset you; I just wanted to let you know that I won't take pictures of you or Thomas anymore if you promise not to contact my family and employer."

"You have my promise. Thank you Mr. Lemmings, I'm glad we could come to an understanding."

Again, I'm sorry for upsetting you. Sometimes my job makes me do things that I'm not proud of."

"I understand. Listen, why don't you give me your card. If I'm in the position to give you a photo op in the future, I'll give you a call."

"Thank you Miss Mills, I would be grateful for any opportunity you could give me," said Lemmings.

Simone thought that she might give him a call when the baby was born, but would the picture be worth anything to him if Thomas didn't acknowledge the child?

****

Martin stopped badgering Simone to tell their mother about the pregnancy; he was dealing with serious problems of his own. He'd proposed to Carly after their most recent argument; fed up, he would've agreed to anything to get her back in his life. But Carly didn't jump into his arms as he'd expected; she turned him down and moved the last of her belongings out of their home.

At twenty weeks pregnant, Simone's belly protruded slightly under her fitted turtleneck, yet she still did not tell her parents about the baby. She had conversations with them over the phone each month, but could not bring herself to discuss the pregnancy. Her father was doing much better; he'd completed his treatments, and the prostate cancer seemed to be in remission. Laura continually reached out to her ex-husband during his illness and, as a result, they were having daily conversations. Hearing this news raised Simone's hopes; here she was, an adult businesswoman living on her own, yet her heart yearned for her parents to live together again.

Her protruding abdomen prompted Simone to shop for maternity clothing. Though she wasn't gaining as much weight as her doctor wanted her to because of the nausea, her current wardrobe couldn't accommodate her new size.

The pregnancy book Nikki had bought for her said expecting mothers must keep their spirits up. Constantly thinking about Thomas and his mother made that extremely challenging. Simone thought that, at the very least, Thomas would call to ask how the pregnancy was progressing. As she shook off the depressing thoughts of Thomas, Simone checked the time because she was taking Nikki out to dinner for her birthday. Last week she'd invited Derrick to come with them to celebrate his cousin's birthday, but he'd never replied back or acknowledged the invite. Derrick had made it clear that their friendship was over.

Simone shook her head as she walked to the Greek restaurant where she was meeting her friend. Nikki loved the Greek specialty Spanakopita; Simone loved it too, but she chose chicken soup and pita chips to avoid the nausea. Simone had been forced to cancel many of their previous Friday night dinners because of her nausea and tonight, she was determined to tough it out and help Nikki celebrate her birthday. After dinner, Simone drove Nikki to an upscale bakery café where the birthday girl ordered a sumptuous caramel layered butterscotch cake with an espresso-flavored glaze, along with a cup of espresso. Simone ordered a plain slice of angel food cake and simple decaffeinated tea. Nikki caught her friend looking long-ingly at the espresso.

"Simone, why don't you take a small sip to satisfy your craving."

Simone sighed. "If only I could. Trust me, you don't want to witness what happens when I drink coffee."

Seeing her friend look worn and tired discouraged Nikki from continuing the celebration. She made up an excuse to cut the outing short because she wanted Simone to go home and get some rest.

For the past week, Dr. Rodsmith's office called repeatedly to book an appointment for Simone to make up for those that she'd missed. They wanted her to come in that day to make up for the previously cancelled appointments, but Simone had planned an afternoon business meeting that she could not reschedule. She promised the doctor she would see her first thing the next morning.

Later that afternoon, Simone locked the shop door and flipped the sign to "Closed." She was so tired that she planned a nap before her dinner. Just as she was turning in, the door buzzer rang. Simone was tempted to not answer but thought it might be important. When she did open the door, she saw Derrick.

"Hi Simone. Hey, you look terrible. Anyway, I wanted to speak to you about your occupancy. I know you are expecting soon; so, I was wondering if you were looking for a larger unit for you and your child to live in. If so, it would be fine with me if you needed to break the lease, I would not hold you to..."

Simone interrupted him, "Derrick, can this wait? I'm not feeling well, I was just about to lie down."

"Well, I wanted to ask you now because I do have someone who's interested..." While Derrick was still talking, Simone's vision became fuzzy and she reached out in vain before collapsing to the floor.

The ambulance came quickly. Derrick went to her bedroom to retrieve her cellphone and handbag; he stayed by her side in the ambulance and called Nikki as soon as the hospital took Simone in.

Nikki arrived promptly and a nurse pointed her in the direction of Simone's room.

"Derrick, what happened to Simone?" she asked when she spotted him in the waiting room.

"I don't know, I was talking to her and she didn't look too good. She said she was tired and didn't feel well, and then as I was talking, she passed out and hit her head."

"Wait, why would you keep talking if she said she didn't feel well? What were you talking about?"

"Well...ah...I was asking if she was looking for a larger unit. You know, for when the baby comes," said Derrick.

"Derrick, I speak to Simone every day. She wasn't planning to move, and you know she would have told you if she were. You just wanted to harass her, didn't you? What is your problem? And how could you just stand there talking while she fainted and hit her head? You should have reached out and caught her when she was falling, you idiot. She could have lost the baby!

"What kind of man are you? Simone is in a situation where she needs her friends, but you've tried your best to make her miserable. Why? Is it because she was interested in another man instead of you? If you really liked Simone, you should have said something over the past year you've been bringing her coffee! You don't wait until she's interested in someone else and then discard her friendship as if *she* did something to *you*. Your behavior has truly shocked me, and I'm embarrassed to be your cousin. You've wronged my friend and I don't even want to look at you now."

Derrick lowered his head remorsefully but Nikki continued, "I'm going to ask the nurse what's going on. You should go home; Simone doesn't need enemies around right now. Give me her purse and phone, I may have to call her family to tell them what has happened." Derrick did as he was told and left in low spirits. Nikki went to the nurse station. After confirming that Simone had allowed them to share her medical condition, she was told that Simone had fainted from dehydration, and that she had a bruise on her head from the fall, but that, thankfully, it wasn't serious.

"Is the baby OK?" Nikki asked.

"Yes, the baby's heartbeat is strong. Poor dear has been crying, thinking she was losing the child, but the baby is fine. Ms. Mills is resting now; please wait a bit before waking her."

"Thank you. If she wakes up, tell her I'll be back soon. I have to make a phone call." Nikki went to her car and pulled out Simone's phone, which she thankfully kept unlocked. She quickly found the contact that she was looking for and was surprised when he picked up.

"Simone?"

"Hello, is this Thomas?"

"Yeah, who's this?" Thomas asked.

"It's Nikki, remember me, I'm Simone's friend?"

"Oh, hello Nikki."

"I was just calling because I thought you would want to know that Simone is in the hospital. She's having complications with the pregnancy. She's worried she may lose the baby, so you may want to tell your mother; though I imagine the two of you would jump for joy if she did lose your child, but I thought it best to notify you anyway.

"You know, Simone is a respectable person and has a good

heart, so she would never make this call. I on the other hand am not so respectable, so I would like to say that you are a low-life maggot; you and your mother can take your 200,000 pounds and stuff it. The two of you are the most miserable people on earth. I curse the day I encouraged my friend to go out with you. Simone has suffered so much because of you and your psycho photographer friend! You are the worst thing that's ever happened to her, you..."

"Nikki! What are you talking about? What pregnancy?"

"Don't act as if you don't know. She called you and you never replied. She sent you a letter to tell you that she was pregnant, but instead of speaking to her yourself, you sent your bitter mother to do your dirty work. What kind of man tells a woman to take 200,000 pounds and go away because he has no interest in his child!"

"This—this isn't true, I never received any letter. We just returned a few days ago from the tour. Where is Simone? I need to see her."

"Why in the world should I tell you where she is? Haven't you hurt her enough?" Nikki asked.

"Nikki, please! Please tell me where she is. I never knew she was pregnant."

"Hmmm, I'll tell you, but if you upset her I'll call security and have you removed. And I don't want your mother within ten miles of my friend. She's at Central Middlesex Hospital, Derrick brought her in this afternoon."

"I'm on my way!" Thomas said.

Nikki left her car and returned to the hospital; she hoped she'd done the right thing by telling Thomas. He genuinely sounded like he hadn't been aware of the pregnancy.

Thomas ran out of his house and sped off for the hospital. Going over in his head the conversation he'd just had with Nikki, he couldn't believe his mother had even spoken to

Simone because he didn't know they'd even met. There must have been some misunderstanding because his mother would have told him of any such letter, he reasoned.

Pregnant? With my *child? Why am I just finding out about this?* he thought. It was then that Thomas remembered the texts and calls he ignored. With a sigh, he realized his not knowing was his fault; he was trying too hard to forget her. It never worked: when Thomas saw the call from her phone, all the feelings he'd been trying to suppress came back immediately. Now, all he could think of was Simone in the hospital, pregnant with his child and having complications.

Thomas arrived at the hospital in record time. He went to the front desk and they told him where Simone was. As he exited the elevator, Thomas spotted Nikki in the waiting area. "Nikki, where is she?" he asked.

"Were you telling the truth? You never received her letter?" she asked.

"No, I did not receive any letter. I've received a few messages asking me to call her, but I was trying to avoid Simone after the breakup. I had no idea she was pregnant."

"Well, you would have known if you called her when she asked you to. So, you have no knowledge of your mother offering her 200,000 pounds?" asked Nikki.

"Of course not! I'm not even sure where she would have gotten 200,000 pounds to offer without me giving her the money," said Thomas.

"Well if I were you, I would check my assets. I'm going to ask the nurse if we can see her now," said Nikki.

"I'll go with you," said Thomas. The nurse saw them coming and got up.

"You can visit for a few minutes but only one at a time, and please don't stay too long. She needs her rest."

"I'll go first," said Nikki.

Simone was awake when Nikki entered. "Hi Nikki," she said weakly. Her voice was hoarse.

"Hi love, you gave me a huge scare," Nikki said as she came to the bed and kissed Simone on the cheek.

"I scared myself; never thought I'd end up in the hospital like this," said Simone.

"Are you feeling better? They said you were crying earlier."

"I was crying, I thought I was losing my baby, but they told me he's doing well. You know, in the beginning I thought of this pregnancy as a burden, but now I don't know what I would do if I lost my baby. I'm so happy he's doing well. The doctor told me that I didn't take my constant nausea serious enough. It was a good thing that Derrick was there, otherwise I could have passed out alone without anyone knowing."

"Hmm, I didn't think of it that way. We will discuss this sometime later but there's someone waiting to see you."

"Oh, is it Derrick? I must have scared him, It's OK to let him in," said Simone.

"No, it's not Derrick, I told him to go home; it's…Thomas." Simone started to protest but Nikki stopped her: "Before you say anything, hear him out. He said he never received your letter because he wasn't back yet and he had no idea that his mother spoke to you."

"Nikki, that doesn't make sense. She was sitting in his house when she said those things to me, how could Thomas not be involved?"

"I don't know Simone, but Thomas seemed genuinely surprised to hear that you were pregnant when I was telling him off, and he came right away. You should see him."

"You can let him in, I'm eager to hear what he has to say," said Simone.

Nikki exited the room and motioned to Thomas to go in. He walked in not knowing what to expect, and they immediately locked eyes as he entered the room. Simone looked frail, and he could tell that she had been crying. Thomas went to the bed and gave her a kiss on the cheek, but when she turned her head away, he was taken aback. "Thomas, why are you here?" she asked.

"Simone, I just returned from the tour a few days ago. I swear, I never received your letter; I had no idea you were pregnant. Nikki told me that you spoke to my mother. Simone, I don't know what my mother was doing; she never called me, and I would never say the things she said to you. I don't understand why she would do that, but I promise you, I'm going to find out." He sat down and took her hand. "Just so you know, I want our child and I want to be a part of their life." Thomas was relieved when she smiled at him.

"I'm so happy to hear that; your mother was so cold. I didn't want to believe that you would say those things, but she was sitting in your house when she said them. She really hurt me, I cried my eyes out that night. I thought you were so angry with me that you wanted nothing to do with our child."

Thomas touched her cheek. "Simone I love you; I would never hurt you even if I were still angry. Tell me what happened, what did the doctor say was wrong?" he asked.

"I had been feeling tired for a while now, but today was really bad. The doctor wanted me to come in a few weeks ago; I kept postponing the appointment because of my business, but I'd planned to see the doctor tomorrow. Today, I was closing the studio when Derrick came by, he was talking to me when I passed out. He called the ambulance and came with me to the hospital. The doctor said I passed out from dehydration, most likely caused by the nausea I experience every morning. It's been hard for me to keep down certain foods, so I haven't been eating as much as I should, and I shouldn't have cancelled my appointments. They're giving me medication and fluids;

I'm feeling better already. They told me the baby is doing well, I just have to increase my weight gain."

Thomas felt guilty, he was the irresponsible one who didn't use a condom the second time they made love, and because of his carelessness, Simone had been suffering with an unplanned pregnancy. He also wasn't happy that Derrick was there for her instead of him. That was his mother's fault, and he planned to deal with her soon. "Simone, I don't know what to say. I want to help in any way I can. You know, when I received the texts and calls from you, I wanted to reply, but I was trying so hard to forget you—forget us. Hearing your voice only made me want to see you.

"Listen, I don't want to tire you out. Please get plenty of rest; I will leave now and come back in the morning. Promise me you'll call if you need anything." At her nod, he kissed her hand and walked out. Then, Thomas found Nikki and thanked her for calling him.

CHAPTER SIXTEEN
MOTHER

Thomas received no response from messages he left demanding his mother to explain what she'd pulled with Simone; he'd also called his brother and grandmother, but neither had heard from her recently. He struggled to believe what Simone had said, though he knew Simone wasn't lying.

He made an urgent appointment with his accountant. Early in his career Thomas had given his mother ordinary power of attorney. Since then, his payables had run smoothly. She paid his bills, took care of work that needed to be done to his house, and looked after his investment properties. She'd done well; but Thomas had a bad feeling about the money offer. When Libby arrived, he questioned her about Simone's visit, and she confirmed his mother's offer of 200,000 pounds for Simone to leave him alone. Libby's confirmation made his heart sink.

"Libby, I need you do me a favor?"

"Sure Thomas, what do you need?"

"Can you call the locksmiths tomorrow? I want them to change the locks to the house. Tell them to give you three sets of keys; you take one and give me two."

"Oh, one for you and your mother?"

"No, one for me and one for Simone. My mother will never get the keys to my house again. While you have them, get them to change the locks at the Colchester house too."

****

Thomas's accountant, Paul, entered the office early to review Thomas's assets before their meeting. He quickly noticed several red flags, making a few calls to the bank as soon as they opened to verify what he saw, as he'd never want to accuse a man's mother of robbing him without proof.

Thomas arrived early, eager to find out what was going on with his assets. Paul didn't waste any time: "Thomas, it's good to see you again, it's been quite some time. Why don't you have a seat and we'll get started. When you called about your problem, I came in early to look over your account and I did find a discrepancy. It's not a huge one and certainly not 200,000 pounds, but it's a monthly amount that dates back for several years."

"What is the amount?" asked Thomas.

"Well, you've been paying 2,689.15 pounds monthly for almost five years. The description for the entry was vague; however, I was able to trace the payments back to a mortgage company. Thomas, you've been paying back a loan you took out for the amount of 250,000.00 pounds. The money was taken out against the value of your home," stated Paul.

Thomas was confused. "I never took out a loan against the equity in any of my properties."

"I know. Your signature wasn't on the papers. Your mother signed as power of attorney," said Paul as he sat back and looked at his client sympathetically.

"I don't understand why she would do this! I would have given her money if she needed it for something."

"Thomas, there's more. The 250,000 pounds was written as a check, which was deposited by a Ms. Judy Marlow."

Thomas was numb. His mother had paid Judy 250,000 pounds almost five years ago, right around the time that Judy left without a reason. Paul gave the visibly shaken Thomas copies of the loan documents and the contact at the bank where his loan had originated. Thomas thanked him and left in a daze.

Sitting in his car, Thomas went over everything in his mind; thinking of the collusion between Judy and his mother made him furious. He couldn't understand why his own mother would do something to hurt him. Suddenly, thoughts of how he used to relieve stress entered his mind for the first time in years; the memories frightened him. He'd never relapsed since leaving rehab four years ago, and he didn't plan to do so now. Thomas immediately called his Narcotics Anonymous sponsor—he needed to talk with someone who understood the mental struggle he was going through.

CHAPTER SEVENTEEN
RECUPERATION

Simone felt so much better, physically and mentally, the second day she spent at the hospital. The fatigue was gone, and she kept down all the food she'd eaten, with the help of the antacid medication her doctor had prescribed. If she managed to keep all of her meals down for another day, she would be approved for discharge with medication. Her spirits were up, too; knowing that Thomas hadn't make that disgusting offer made her so much happier. She wanted her child, which a sonogram had revealed was a boy, to know his father. Simone also wanted to believe that Thomas would never intentionally hurt her.

She called Martin and told him she was in the hospital. Martin implored her to tell their parents what was going on, but Simone insisted the news still had to wait. Her doctor had told her that stress could increase her nausea, and making that call would be very stressful for her. Despite pleas reassuring Martin that she would be fine, he booked a flight. She would be seeing him in five days.

Becky visited with her in the morning and offered to take Simone home when she was discharged. Becky also said she would to spend the day with Simone to make sure she was taken care of.

Nikki also came to check on Simone later in the day. "Hey, Derrick's still upset with himself for letting you fall; he wants to know if there's anything he can do to help with your business, he also said to forget about this month's rent."

"Tell him not to worry about the fall, neither of us knew I was going to pass out," said Simone.

Thomas arrived in the late afternoon looking very distraught. He came over and kissed her on the forehead before sitting down.

"How are you feeling today?" he asked.

"Looks like I'm feeling better than you are. Thomas, what happened? You look terrible!"

"I should have called you earlier. I'm sorry I didn't come this morning, but I found out some disturbing news about my mother and I'm struggling to deal with it. You don't know this, but I was going to marry someone about five years ago; this was before I went to rehab. Judy and I were addicts; we got high together, but I loved her and I wanted us to get married.

"I had asked my mother to help Judy with the wedding arrangements. About a week later Judy called off the wedding and refused to see me to talk it over. I never knew why she cancelled the wedding, and that devastated me; I sunk deeper into my addiction after that. It destroyed my heart and my confidence. All I could think of was that the woman I wanted no longer wanted me. Anyway, I found out this morning that my mother took out a loan against my home for 250,000 pounds the same week Judy left me. This morning my accountant showed me proof that Judy was the recipient of the money. My mother paid Judy to leave me, just like she tried to pay you off. I have been looking for her, calling her, with no response. I've also told my grandmother everything and she's trying to track her down too.

"My accountant audited all my assets. In addition to the loan, my mother has increased her spending considerably; I had no choice but to remove her name from all my finances. What I don't understand is that I've given her practically everything she wanted, and instead of looking out for my happiness, she's been stealing from me and ruining my relationships. How could my own mother do this to me?"

Simone's heart went out to Thomas, he was so dejected. "Thomas, I'm so sorry for what you're going through; maybe in her mind, she was looking out for you, but she didn't take into consideration how you would feel."

"I can't believe you're saying this. After the way she treated you, you're giving her the benefit of doubt?"

Thomas looked so miserable; Simone wanted to cheer him up. "Listen, let's take our minds off our headaches and think about something else," said Simone.

"Something else like what?" he asked.

"Here, take a look at these. I was thinking of names for our son." Simone handed him her tablet with a list of names for the baby.

Thomas looked at the list and frowned. "Keanu, Orion, Leslie? You can't be serious; these are not proper names for a boy."

"They don't have to be proper, he's our child and we can name him whatever we want," said Simone.

"Do you want our son to come home crying every day because someone made fun of his name?" asked Thomas.

"Thom, you're being overly dramatic, no one will make him cry because of his name."

Thomas loved when Simone unconsciously called him

Thom. He still remembered her calling him Thom the night they'd made love.

"Simone, I want to ask you something. I want you to stay with me when you leave here. I promise I won't bother you. You can stay on the other side of the house; I just want to make sure you're safe and well cared for. Libby will take care of all your meals; and we'll make sure to fatten you up so the doctor will be pleased."

"Thomas, I believe you've fattened me up enough," said Simone. They both laughed.

"I made keys for you," Thomas said, but he saw the laughter leave her face. "Wait, don't say no yet; just think about it. Here are the keys. Even if you don't want to stay, I want you to feel comfortable to come whenever you want. Promise me you'll think about it."

Simone didn't reply. Thomas giving her the keys reminded her of Henri and how he'd used her. Still, that relationship had ended badly because there was no future in it: Henri was already married. Thomas wasn't married, but he'd only asked her to live with him. On the other hand, he was willing to marry Judy, a lady he was getting high with. Simone sadly concluded that her one mistake would keep her forever connected to a man who had no intention of marrying her.

Before Simone could think of a way to give back the keys, Thomas's phone rang, "Hi Gran, no, she never returned my calls. Sure, I'll be there tonight, see you then." Then he explained to Simone, "My grandmother had a meeting with my mother. She wants me to come over to discuss the conversation with me. This should be very interesting. I want to hear what my mother had to say for herself, but I can't see how I can forgive her for what she did to you—to us. I'm going to leave now but I'll be back tomorrow. Let me know when you're to be sent home; I'll take you to whichever home you want to

go to, just promise me you'll take better care of your health."
When she agreed, Thomas leaned over and kissed Simone on
the cheek before he left.

Simone waved goodbye with a smile on the outside. On the
inside she was trying to control her feelings again. She'd love
to live in Thomas's house, but she knew her willpower wasn't
strong enough to stay out of his bed.

The nurse brought her dinner, lasagna and steamed vegetables. Simone had no problem eating the vegetables, but the
lasagna was the type of dish that made her queasy. She forced
herself to eat the cheese- and sauce-laden meal; this time the
food stayed down without any nausea. Elated, Simone smiled
as she continued the meal, knowing this feat kept her on track
to be discharged soon.

CHAPTER EIGHTEEN
MRS. ELIZABETH LLOYD

Thomas parked outside his grandmother's house, a historic stone building with a thatched roof. The well-maintained garden welcomed visitors to the front door. He rang the bell and waited patiently for the elderly matriarch to let him in. At the door, his grandmother gave Thomas the usual long hug and kiss. They sat down in the sitting room and she took his hands in hers. "Thom, first I want to say that your mother loves you very much. She was always more concerned with you than James because you took your father's death so hard. Her only fault is that she also has a love for money.

"Do you remember when James found out you were snorting cocaine? I had a nasty row with her after you left that day because I realized it was only me and your brother telling you to give up the drugs. I questioned her on it and she became very upset. You see, your mother loved the lifestyle you'd provided her too much; I believe she never told you to stop the drugs because she was afraid you would cut her off financially. Anyway, that day, I accused her of putting money before you. I said nothing to you because that argument was just between me and your mum.

"Your mother has made some terrible mistakes concerning you and your assets, but her heart was initially in the right place. I did not know Judy; what I knew about her, I didn't like. James didn't take to her, either, but he kept his mouth shut because he didn't want you to kick him out of your life altogether. He loves you. Remember, you're James's little brother; he was raised to look out for you. But when you pulled away from us it truly hurt him, though he never said anything to you. You know, your brother is big and burly, he likes to act tough, but his heart is softer than yours. Anyway, your mother felt the same way about Judy that James did, so she hired an investigator to check her out. The investigator discovered that Judy wasn't seeing you exclusively, she was also sleeping with your drug dealer. It may have been some sort of payment relationship, I don't know, but the fact remains that we knew you didn't know what was going on. When she found out, your mother took it upon herself to test Judy's love for you. So, she withdrew the 250,000 pounds and arranged a meeting with Judy. She told her she knew about her other boyfriend and then she offered Judy the money to get out of your life. Judy took the money.

"Today your mother told me she made the money offer to Simone because she thought Simone was just after your money, too. She came to this conclusion after she saw Simone in the papers leaving your house alone that morning. Your mother wants to apologize to you for that, she said she was just looking out for you. I know you told me she's taking out more money than what you originally agreed to give her; it's possible she got carried away with living a certain lifestyle. I asked her to stay and explain everything herself, but she's afraid to face you.

"Thom, I'm ashamed of how your mother has represented the Lloyd family to Simone. If you think she'll see me, I would like to visit her tomorrow to apologize for what your mother has done, and to welcome her into the family. I'm really looking forward to holding your first child," she said with a warm smile.

Thomas was stunned by the information his grandmother had relayed; it was confirmation that Judy had walked out of his life for money. He'd believed their relationship was strong, though now he realized his view of that relationship had been through a haze of drugs. Thomas knew he'd loved Judy; there was just no confirmation that she'd loved him.

"She's afraid to face me? The son she 'was looking out for?'" Thomas shook his head. "I'll deal with my mother later. Simone's my main concern now. Gran, your meeting Simone is a good idea. Call my driver in the morning when you're ready for him. As for my mum, the next time you see her, tell her she needs to meet me face to face to resolve this. Maybe she meant well when she offered Judy the money, but it was still my money and my relationship. I'm a grown man, I have the right to choose who I want to be with regardless of how she feels. When Judy left me so abruptly, I almost destroyed myself with drugs; so, in the end, her actions didn't help me. She's my mother, and I will always love her, but she'll never have authority over my assets, or keys to my properties, ever again. My mother has taught me to never trust her."

CHAPTER NINETEEN
FAMILY HOME

It was an eventful day for Simone; in the morning, the nurse brought her a full breakfast with instructions for her to eat everything. Though she felt bloated afterwards, there were thankfully no signs of nausea. A few of her friends from church came to visit; they brought flowers and prayers for her to get better. Derrick arrived with a huge bouquet of flowers, greeting her with a kiss on the cheek.

"Simone, I'm so upset with myself for letting you fall. I'm sorry for being angry with you, I had no right."

"Derrick, why were you angry with me? Did I insult you in some way?"

"No, you had nothing to do with it. This is sort of embarrassing, but I thought you knew how I felt about you. In the beginning when we'd have coffee together, I thought, *This is nice, Simone's a great friend*; however, by the time summer came around my feelings began to change. I wanted more than friendship with you, but I knew you weren't thinking of me in that way. So, I was hoping, apparently in vain, that with our continued Friday meetings you'd start developing feelings for me. After Nikki told me off, I realized that I should have said something sooner, and not assumed you knew how I felt.

"When I saw you with those men, I didn't realize they were all Thomas. It seemed to me that you were interested in anyone but me; that made me angry. Then Nikki told me you were seeing Thomas Lloyd. I thought, what chance do I have with you now? He's a rich rockstar. In my mind, I believed you wouldn't allow yourself to be with someone like me, because someone like Thomas was a better catch. I remembered all the things you said to me about being a Christian, and then you were pregnant; and I just got angrier because I thought you were a hypocrite. Seeing you with Thomas was torturous; all I could think was you should have been with me, not him. I raised the rent and harassed you about moving because I couldn't take it anymore.

"I was harassing you when you passed out and you scared me to death. I knew you didn't love me, and I was wrong for being angry with you because you fell for someone else. Simone, can you forgive me?"

"Of course I forgive you. I understand now what you were thinking, but you should have told me how you felt."

"How can you be so forgiving Simone? I treated you poorly," lamented Derrick.

"Derrick, if I'm calling myself a Christian, and Christ forgives me for having sex without marriage, how can I not forgive you? Who am I to hold onto unforgiveness? I'm just happy I won't be seeing your angry scowl again," she said laughingly.

Derrick laughed too and said, "Was it that bad?"

"I wish you could have seen your reflection. You reminded me of Barnabas from Dark Shadows." They both laughed again.

"Simone, if there's anything you need, please let me know. I want you to know that I'm here for you. I'll always be your friend."

Simone noticed an elderly, white-haired lady with a cane in the doorway and she called out, "Hello?"

"Hello dear, I'm so sorry to disturb you. I'm Thomas's grandmother. I just wanted to visit with you for a few minutes, is this a bad time?"

Derrick rose up from the chair. "Simone, I should be going now. Give me a call when they discharge you, I would be happy to take you home."

"Thanks Derrick, and thank you for coming by." Derrick kissed her on the forehead.

"Oh dear, I hope I didn't cut your visit short," stated Thomas's grandmother.

"It's not a problem ma'am, I have to get back to work anyway. Here, let me help you to the chair," suggested Derrick.

"Thank you young man," she said as Derrick assisted her to the seat. Derrick waved goodbye to Simone when he left.

"I hope you forgive me for interrupting your visit with that young man, but I was determined to come down here to apologize," said Mrs. Lloyd.

"I don't understand, what do you have to apologize for?" asked Simone.

"Well, I wanted to apologize for the insult my daughter-in-law gave you. You should know that she acted on her own; she in no way represents the feelings of the Lloyds. We are very happy that Thomas has found someone to love and we're overjoyed that he will soon be a father. You don't know how long I've been praying for him to find a good woman. Now I believe my prayers were answered."

Simone blushed and said, "Well, I don't know if your prayers were answered, but I do love him." Simone and Mrs. Lloyd continued their discussion. Mrs. Lloyd told Simone stories about Thomas when he was a little boy, and then she told her what happened when her son, Thomas's father, died.

"That was a terrible, terrible time; we all cried until we couldn't cry anymore. He was my only child. My son had a friendly, good heart and he loved his boys. Thomas favors him a great deal. My son and Thomas's mom married early at eighteen; they decided to take a loan and open a retail store. My son worked long hours, yet he always had time for his family on Sunday afternoons. The boys would look forward to their time with him after church. Then one day he was taken from us; just like that, my son was dead. It's true when they say burying your child is the hardest thing you could ever imagine.

"The boys kept me going; I had to make sure they were raised properly since their father was no longer around; so, I moved in to take care of them while their mother worked in the store. I trust I did a good job, except for Thomas's stubbornness. You see, Thomas was only seven at the time of his father's death. He took it very hard and vowed never to go to church or pray again because God let his father die. At first I thought, he's young and upset, he'll forget this silly vow and go back to church; but he never did. When he came home from rehab, I tried to steer him towards my church, to no avail. Anyway, enough talking about the negative; let me show you pictures of his brother and his family; they would like to meet you, too. Your child has three cousins. This is James and his wife, Sarah, and these are the children," she said as she pointed to the photos. Simone enjoyed looking at Thomas's family; she remembered seeing his niece and nephew in the photo he'd texted her.

"Listen dear, I promised Thomas I wouldn't stay too long because you need your rest, but it's been a pleasure speaking with you. I hope you don't mind, but I want to give you something." She reached into her bag and took out a small velvet box. Mrs. Lloyd opened the box to reveal a small gold cross on a chain. "My late husband and I gave this to Thomas when he was born. His brother received one too. I want you to have this for your son."

"Oh, Mrs. Lloyd, are you sure? Thank you so much." Simone opened her arms and she and Mrs. Lloyd embraced. "This is so sweet of you to do for the baby."

"Nonsense, I'm passing it down to the next generation and I want to thank you for letting there be another generation. Thank you so much for carrying my great grandchild." She bent closer and kissed Simone on the cheek. "Now I must leave because you and the baby must rest." She waved goodbye with her cane before walking away; leaving Simone in good spirits. It felt nice to know that her son would have other loving family members who would welcome him.

****

As planned, the doctor approved Simone's discharge in the morning, after giving her instructions to change her diet to increase weight gain. Becky had called earlier and confirmed she was on her way to take her home and stay with her for the day. As she waited, Simone decided to call Thomas and fill him in on the visit with his grandmother. "Hi, Thomas, did I wake you?"

"No, I was already up. I'm in the garden now. How are you feeling today?"

"I'm 100% better, they're discharging me soon, but you don't have to worry about picking me up because Becky is coming for me. I was calling you about your grandmother; Thomas, she is so sweet and caring, I love her."

"I'm glad you two hit it off so well. She called me yesterday to tell me how much she liked you; hope she didn't stay too long, she loves to talk you know."

"No, she didn't stay too long. She came just as Derrick was

leaving and she left about twenty minutes later; I really enjoyed her visit."

"That's nice, uh, why was Derrick there?" asked Thomas.

"Oh, Derrick came by to apologize for not catching me when I fainted, and he said some other things."

"Other things? What other things?" asked Thomas. Simone suddenly regretted mentioning Derrick but figured she might as well get this over with.

"Derrick told me he's been in love with me, and he was waiting for me to feel the same way. You were right, I was oblivious to his feelings; it never crossed my mind that he felt that way about me."

"So, how do you feel about your landlord, who lives next door, being in love with you?" Thomas asked.

"It is somewhat awkward now. I guess we'll never meet for Friday morning coffee again, I'm going to miss that," she said sadly.

Not liking what he was hearing, Thomas suggested some changes. "Simone, you must move out of his building. It would be best for you and Derrick; besides, you'll need more space when the baby comes."

"I don't know Thomas, I have so much on my plate right now, and the business has been picking up lately. Packing up to move is the last thing on my mind."

"I wouldn't let you lift a finger. I will hire professional movers and I'll obtain the new business space for you. Just tell me when you're ready."

"Thanks for the offer Thomas, I'll think about it."

****

Though she had received excellent care from the hospital, it felt good to be home. Simone planned to open the shop and stay at her desk, but Becky told her to stay in bed with her laptop since she'd just come home from the hospital. Simone's friend was cooking a wonderful chicken stew when Thomas called to say he was coming over later. Becky set up a tray with the stew for Simone before leaving to pick up Simone's groceries.

"Hello? Simone? It's me, Thomas," he called out when he entered the shop.

"I'm in the back." Simone walked out to meet him in the studio. As he greeted her with a hug and kiss on the cheek, Simone wondered if she'd ever reach the point where her heart didn't react to his touch.

"I've got a surprise for you, just wait here," he said. Thomas propped the door open and waved for someone to come. Two men carried in a huge lounge chair, setting it down next to Simone's desk and plugging it into a nearby outlet.

"Thomas, what did you do?" asked Simone. When the men told Thomas that the chair was ready, he took Simone by the hand and made her sit in it. One of the men handed him a remote and Thomas then pushed one of the buttons. The chair moved Simone into a lounge position with her legs lifted and the back of the chair tilted down.

"It's a state-of-the-art zero-gravity chair; it lightens the pressure on your back and legs and puts you in a relaxed position. The salesman said it's great for pregnant women, how does it feel?"

"It feels wonderful, I could easily fall asleep in this chair; thanks Thom, this was very thoughtful of you."

"Anything for you luv," Thomas replied. The two men left the studio and returned with two huge standing bouquets of flowers which they placed against the wall of her office.

"Thomas, are those for me?"

"Of course, I was going to have them delivered to your

hospital room, but I wasn't sure when you were going to be released."

"They're gorgeous, thank you so much," she said as she stood up and gave him a hug.

Becky returned through the open door with groceries. "Becky, I'm glad you're here, I want you to meet Thomas."

"Hello Becky, it's nice to meet you; let me help you with your bags."

"Thank you Thomas, it's nice to meet you, too." They went to the kitchen with the bags, and Becky proceeded to put the groceries away.

After assisting Becky, Thomas returned to Simone. "I see that you are in good hands today, so I will come by tomorrow to check on you. Please call me if you need anything at all." He leaned over and kissed her lightly on the lips before leaving. Simone smiled as he left but her smile slowly turned into a worried expression.

Becky returned and said, "Simone I've stored everything away. I marked the description of the different meals in the containers."

"Thanks Becky. You've been a great help—I don't know what I would have done without you."

"Nonsense, I see that you have people who are looking out for you. Nikki called to check on you, your landlord, Derrick, asked if you needed anything, and you also have the handsome Thomas looking out for you. You're going to be just fine." Becky paused, then continued: "But why do you seem so worried?"

"I'm worried about Thomas. Even though I broke off our relationship, he treats me as if we're still dating. He just kissed me on the lips when he said goodbye. I've been trying so hard to push my feelings for him away because I know we have to keep our relationship platonic, but it's harder than I imagined."

"Simone, he's a sweet man and I can tell that he likes being with you. Does he understand why you can't live with him?"

"I told him but I don't think he takes me seriously. He offered me the keys to his house and told me I could come whenever I wanted. What I don't understand is why he only wants me to live with him, when just five years ago he asked his girlfriend to marry him.

"I'm also thinking of my brother; he'll arrive in a few days. I know he wants me to move back to New York. This business has been a dream of mine for so long. Though I still have a loan to pay off, sales are picking up now. Logically, selling is not a good idea, but I've been thinking about what Martin said; maybe the only way to stay away from Thomas is to sell the business and move home. The problem with that is, it would hurt him. He's looking forward to co-raising our child, and I want my son to have a good relationship with his father."

"That's a difficult decision, and I would hate to see you leave. The two of you must sit down together and discuss this before you make any decisions concerning the baby. Maybe, when he truly knows how you feel, he will offer to marry you."

"Becky, I don't want him to feel as though he must marry me to keep his son in his life. I can't imagine going through life knowing my husband married me under duress."

"Simone, I know from experience that raising a child as a single parent is very difficult. You need to pray about this, and you should read **Isaiah 42:16**. That verse explains that God will make a way when there seems to be no way."

"You're right, I do need to pray about it because right now I can't see how any of my plans will work out."

Later that afternoon, Simone was thinking about what to do when she decided it was time to make the long overdue call. "Hi, Mom."

"Hi, Simone, I haven't heard from you in a while, where have you been?"

"Mom, that's part of the reason why I'm calling you."

"Simi, what is it?"

"Mom, are you sitting down?"

"Simone you're scaring me; please tell me what's wrong."

"Mom...I'm pregnant."

"Simone!"

"I'm sorry Mom, I know you're disappointed and—"

"Wait Simone...this is a shock, and I wasn't expecting this from you...but it's alright."

Simone was confused as she still remembered her mother's reaction to Henri—she'd expected her mother to scream at her now, at the very least. "Mom, did you just say it's alright?"

Her mother sighed and said, *"Simone, you've been shutting me out of your personal life since we had that argument about the professor you slept with. You never tell me your plans or who you're dating. When you decided to stay in London, you didn't include me or your father in those considerations. Simi, I shouldn't have said those mean things before you left for London. I was comparing what you did to what Cindy did, and I shouldn't have. You were young and had just turned eighteen; your professor took advantage of your innocence, and I know you didn't know he was married. I should have argued with the school for allowing the professor to take advantage of you as his student. I'm so sorry, sweetheart, I never meant to hurt you."*

Simone was in tears. "Thanks Mom," was all she could get out.

"You don't have to thank me, I should have apologized a long time ago; I just didn't know how. You're a grown woman and though I would have liked you to be married first before you became pregnant, I know these things happen. Is the father your friend Thomas? How far along are you?"

"I'm 21 weeks pregnant and yes, he is the father."

"Simone, that's five months! I wished you would have told me sooner. Wait a minute, that means you were pregnant when you came home for Christmas?"

"I found out that week, but I wasn't certain until I came back and saw a doctor. I didn't tell you earlier because I know you would have told Dad and I didn't want to stress him out while he was receiving his treatments."

"Honey, I don't know what to say. You're probably right, I would have told him if you didn't. What does your boyfriend plan to do?"

"Mother, he's not exactly my boyfriend. I broke up with him in November so we're just friends now. He wanted me to move in with him but I told him no. I'm not really sure what is going to happen. Martin suggested I move back to New York with you."

"Simone, that would be wonderful, you know I'd love to have you here."

"I haven't made up my mind yet Mom. I'm just thinking about it for now. I have to consider my business, my loan, and my lease with Derrick."

"Simone, why don't I come and stay with you for a little while."

"I would like that Mom, but maybe closer to the due date. I'll need all the help you can give me when the baby comes."

"Oh, I'm definitely coming then, but that's four months away."

"Alright Mom, maybe some time after Martin leaves; he arrives in a few days."

"You already told Martin, didn't you! I wondered why he suddenly wanted to see you. You two should not be keeping these types of secrets from me and your father."

"Mom, please don't blame Martin; he wanted me to tell you earlier, I was the one who insisted I wait. I'm sorry, one thing led to another and the time just went by. I was nauseous for a long time; in fact, I was in the hospital this week, but I'm better now."

"Simone, I can't believe you were in the hospital and never called me or your father. What happened?"

"It was nothing serious, I was a little dehydrated."

"Please, please, don't keep secrets from us anymore. What if something serious had happened?"

"You're right, I should have told you earlier. I promise, no more secrets." The door to her shop opened. "Mom, a customer is here, I have to go now but I'll call you when Martin arrives."

****

Martin called as he exited Heathrow Airport to let Simone know he was on his way. She'd planned to pick him up, but he told her not to worry. Simone was in the backyard tending to her herb plants when she heard the doorbell and she immediately started running towards the door but slowed herself down when she remembered that the doctor had told her to take it easy. When she opened the door, Simone was shocked to see her mother standing next to Martin.

"Mom! You're...you—you should have told me you were coming with Martin," she said as she hugged them both.

"I wasn't sure if I could make it on the same flight! I had to fly standby because I booked so late. Let me look at you; honey, you don't look that pregnant," said Laura.

Laura and Simone discussed all aspects of the pregnancy before chatting about everything back in the States. For the first time in years, Simone was homesick.

Simone soon learned that her father had stayed with her mother for a few days during a recent business trip and he had since started the process of transferring his job back to the New York area. Laura appeared happy about the prospect; and, noticing her mother's reaction, Simone raised an eyebrow as she and Martin exchanged glances.

Afterwards, Laura decided to take a nap, as the long flight had tired her out. Martin didn't waste time: he immediately asked to see Simone's accounts and loan documents. A few hours passed before he was satisfied with his review.

"Simone, you'll still have 25,000 pounds left on your loan after applying your assets. Dad and I can help you out with that...unless your lover boy is in a position to help pay back the loan?"

"Martin, please don't call Thomas names. I spoke with him when I was in the hospital and he told me that he'd never received my letter and that his mother made the offer all on her own. Thomas was very upset with her," said Simone.

"Still sounds like a crazy family to me. Why did she even offer you the money? How much was it, by the way?" asked Martin.

"She offered me 200,000 pounds."

"What! Was it a serious offer?"

"Martin!"

"Well, was it?"

"Sort of. Based on her past dealings, it's clear she would have given me the money," said Simone.

"Who are these people. Are they rich or something?" asked Martin. Simone brought him to her laptop, Googled *Thomas Lloyd*, and showed Martin the screen.

"That's your Thomas! Thomas Lloyd from Access?"

"Yeah, that's him."

"I know him— Well, I mean, I have some of his music on my playlists. Wasn't he arrested for drug possession in Japan?

Doesn't he have a really bad drug habit? How in the world did you two meet?"

"That's a very long story—and he hasn't had that habit since he finished rehab," said Simone.

"Sounds to me like you're still keeping secrets."

"Martin, I'm not intentionally keeping secrets; I just didn't think some information was important to bring up."

"So, what does Thomas Lloyd think about you having his child?"

"He wants the baby, and he want to be an active father. He's even given me the keys to his

house and offered to let me live there."

"Well, to me it sounds like he's trying to do the right thing. Why did you guys break up? Did he do something?"

"Martin, you know I don't believe in premarital sex." Martin gave her a funny look. "Yes, I know I'm pregnant, but I never planned to sleep with Thomas. In fact, the night we had sex I was planning to break up with him because I knew we were heading in that direction. Then I made a mistake."

"Are you in love with him?"

"Yes, that's why I'm considering moving back home. If I leave, I won't be tempted to do this again."

"Really? This Christian thing is very confusing. Does he love you?" asked Martin.

"Yes, I think he does."

"OK, you love him, he loves you, and you're having his baby. So why don't you get married?"

"Thomas hasn't asked me to marry him, he's only asked me to move in with him."

"Maybe I should have a talk with him."

"No Martin, I don't want anyone pressuring him to marry me, and I don't want to be with anyone who was forced to marry me."

"Simone, you're being unreasonable. Look, you're my sister; I'll explain to him that Dad and I don't want you to just live with anyone, and that he should marry you if he wants to live with you."

"Martin, how would you feel if Carly's father or brother said that to you? Tell me something: you love Carly and Carly loved you; the two of you lived together for five years! Why didn't you ask her to marry you during that time?"

"Simone, I don't want to talk about Carly now."

"Well, I'll tell you why: you were selfish. You had all the comforts of marriage without the commitment. You knew Carly wanted to have children but you didn't want to because you were comfortable. You love her, but you didn't care how she felt."

"That's not true, I do care. it's just that...well, when Mom and Dad broke up, it shocked me. I thought they would be together forever. So many people get divorced after marriage; I figured, what's the point? Anyway, I did offer to marry her in the end," said Martin.

"Martin, you asked her to marry you only after she asked *you* several times, gave up, and moved out. Your offer made her feel like you were doing her a favor. No woman wants that—a woman wants a man to desire marriage with her. Did you express any desire, Martin?"

Martin hung his head low. "Simone, you're right. I didn't propose the right way, I messed up."

"Martin, Carly loves you; it's not too late."

"She ignores all my texts and calls, what else can I do?" he said.

"Was that really your best effort? Did you send a letter or flowers? Did you speak to one of her parents? I'm guessing the answer is no. If you really want to win Carly back, you have to fight for her. Try harder; be sincere when you speak to her.

Carly invested five years of her life into a relationship with you, make her believe she didn't waste her time." Simone thought for a moment, then continued: "Oh! I know what you can do. You can write her a letter that expresses how you feel. I'll help in any way I can."

"Alright Simi," Martin sighed, "I'll take all the help I can get."

Just then, Simone's phone rung. "Hi Thomas."

"Hi Simone, I wanted to check on you, how are you feeling today?"

"I'm feeling much better, thanks for calling."

"Great, would you be up to going out for dinner tonight?"

"I can't tonight, my mother and brother flew in today. We'll probably go out later after Mom's recovered from the flight."

"Hey, why don't I come over, get to know your family, and take everyone out to dinner later, how's that?"

"Sure Thomas, that sound fine."

"Great, I'll be over in a little while."

"Martin that was Thomas. He's coming over later, and he's taking us out to dinner when Mom wakes up. Please promise you'll will not say anything about marriage."

"I don't know Simone, maybe you and Mom should go without me. I'm not sure I want to have dinner with your friend."

"Martin he's the father of your nephew, you'll have to talk to him at some point."

"Well if you move back home, I won't have to deal with him at all."

"Martin, Thomas is not a bad person—"

"Simone stop. No matter what you say I'll always know him as the guy who got my little sister pregnant. He'll never be a great guy in my eyes. I think I'll just leave before he gets here."

"Martin you're overreacting."

"Listen, you don't want me to tell him what's on my mind; my not being around him is the only way I can honor your wish."

"Martin you just got here, I don't want you to leave. I'll call him back and cancel."

"No, you and Mom go to dinner. I'll be at the pub; I feel like a beer right now anyway. Maybe I can convince Derrick to come with me."

After Martin left, Simone went to her bedroom to change her outfit. Laura woke up when she heard Simone moving in the room.

"Sorry Mom, I didn't mean to wake you."

"Don't worry about me, I didn't want to sleep too long since I do have to adjust to the time here. What are you and Martin doing?"

"Martin went to find Derrick to go to the pub."

"How is Derrick? He's such a nice young man," said Laura.

"Derrick is fine. He's actually the one who took me to the hospital when I wasn't well."

"I'm glad you mentioned the hospital, I want you to tell me everything."

"I'll be happy to, but right now you should get ready for dinner. Thomas is going to take us out; he called when you were asleep, and he's on his way now."

"Why didn't you wake me earlier? I haven't had time to unpack!"

"Mom, take your time, I told him I wasn't leaving until you were rested, so he's happy to hang out here until you're ready."

"I don't like to have people waiting for me; I'll be ready soon," said Laura.

"Mom please take your time. I'll be back, there's someone at the door."

Simone opened the door to let Thomas in. After surveying

the room and seeing that they were alone, he pulled her close and tried to kiss her on the mouth, but she turned her head, and his kiss fell on her cheek.

"Simone, why did you do that?" asked Thomas. Before she could answer Laura came into the room. She saw Thomas's arm around Simone's waist before Simone quickly backed out of his arms.

"Hello, you must be Thomas," said Laura.

"Yes ma'am," Thomas said as he walked over to Simone's mother to shake her hand. "It's a pleasure to meet you, Mrs. Mills."

"It's nice to finally meet you too," said Simone's mother. Just then her cellphone rang; she excused herself and took the call. "Hello? Oh, Martin why are you calling? Why don't you come back? What's that? You're with Derrick... Oh, that's wonderful news. I'll tell Simone, please tell Derrick thank you for me, goodbye."

Laura returned to the others and explained, "Simone, that was Martin. He's with Derrick at the pub. He asked him if you could break your lease so that you could move back to New York and Derrick said not to worry about it. Isn't that wonderful!"

"Wait—you're moving back to New York? When did you decide this, and why haven't you told me you're leaving?" asked Thomas.

"I haven't decided anything yet. I was going to tell you that I was thinking about it."

"Why would you leave London? What's going to happen to us—and our child?" asked Thomas. When Laura saw Thomas's reaction, she realized she'd said too much; she also noted that he didn't seem to be behaving like a man who was no longer in a relationship with her daughter.

"Simone, I'm still a little tired, maybe it's best if the two of you have dinner alone together," suggested Laura.

"Are you sure Mom? You haven't been out since you came. I'll stay with you tonight; Thomas and I can speak tomorrow."

"Simone I'll be fine; I don't want to ruin your evening. The two of you should go. Thomas, it was very nice to meet you."

"Thank you Mrs. Mills, it was a pleasure to meet you too, and I hope to see you again before you leave," said Thomas as he took Simone's arm and ushered her out the door. Simone noticed his expression was very serious.

"Thomas, maybe we should discuss this after you've calmed down." She received no reply. He waited until Simone had her seat belt on before backing the Porsche out of the parking spot and accelerating the vehicle down the road at a high speed. "Thomas, why are you driving so fast?"

He sighed and slowed the speed. "I drive fast when I'm angry. Sorry, I didn't mean to frighten you."

After they reached their destination in Kensington, Thomas spoke with the Maître d', who called over a waiter to escort them to a private room that Thomas had previously reserved for Simone's family. The waiter ushered them to a booth and Simone sat first before Thomas seated himself next to her. Simone felt trapped, she wished they were sitting near the other guests as she didn't want to be alone with Thomas at that moment. The waiter took their order and returned with their beverages.

After the waiter left, Thomas began. "We need to talk," he said as he turned toward her in the booth. "Please tell me why you're leaving London."

"I haven't made that decision yet. Martin suggested that it would better for me if I came home and raised our child there."

"How could you do that? I wouldn't be able to see you or the baby."

"Thomas, we're not together. Remember? We broke up before you went on tour."

"Simone, we both know that you broke up with me because you were upset that we had sex. I thought we were moving past that. Don't you think it's best for our child if his parents raise him together? I don't want to lose you, and I don't want to lose my child."

"Thomas, you'll never lose your child; we would work something out, I promise."

"Why can't we work *us* out? You said you loved me, why can't we live together?" he implored as he leaned in closer to her.

Simone pushed him away. "Thomas, we can't be together because you don't respect who I am. You want things your way and I can't live like that; I can't live your lifestyle. I never hid my faith from you yet you keep asking me to live with you."

"Again with your faith? Why can't you let yourself be free, like before?" suggested Thomas.

"I shouldn't have done what I did before, and now I'm going to regret it for the rest of my life. I never planned to be a single parent, much less as I was just getting my business off the ground."

"So you're moving because of money? You need money for your business? I can give you money."

"No Thomas, it's not about money. I'm not asking for any and I don't need your money." Simone was upset and frustrated. "Thomas, I need to get up." After he honored her request, Simone took her purse and slid out of the booth.

"Where are you going? We haven't had dinner yet. Can't we talk some more?"

"I'm not hungry anymore, I'm just tired. We've talked, but you're not hearing me, or you don't want to relate to what I'm saying. You're belittling my values to bully me into living the way you want me to. I love you with all my heart; I think of you every day, but I can't live the way you want me to. There is no future for us, we're just too different.

"It will be difficult, but we'll have to co-parent our child without being together."

Thomas seemed stunned, so she kissed him goodbye on the cheek. "I'll text you my next sonogram appointment so that you can see the baby." With that, Simone walked out of the restaurant without looking back.

On her ride home in a taxi, Simone replayed their argument in her head. She'd hoped Thomas would understand what she needed to continue their relationship; unfortunately, tonight proved she had to move on with her life. Even knowing it was the right decisions, she felt as if she was breaking her own heart again by pushing Thomas away for the second and final time. It had been eight years since Henri. She'd waited so long to fall in love again, and to have that person love her back. This time he was at least unmarried, but Thomas, just like Henri, offered no commitment.

When the taxi pulled up in front of her home, Simone dried her tears before entering so her mother wouldn't realize that she wasn't happy. Laura was up and watching TV when she walked in.

"That was a fast dinner Simone, how was it?"

"I wasn't very hungry and I'm tired, I'll turn in early for bed." Simone tried her best to avoid eye contact with her mom. Laura was to sleep in the bedroom with her so she couldn't allow herself to cry in bed tonight.

The next morning, Simone woke up to the smells of a wonderful breakfast. She walked into the kitchen and saw that her mother had cooked all of Simone's favorite foods: cheese grits, buttermilk biscuits, honeyed ham; all the foods her Southern grandmother use to make. Simone walked over, hugged Laura from behind and said, "Thanks Mom."

"You're welcome Simi, now hurry and wash up, the food is almost ready." When Simone came back to the kitchen her mother said, "Should we wake up Martin and wait for him to get ready?"

"No, let him sleep; I'm not eating cold grits because Martin decided to spend all night drinking beer with Derrick when he was supposed to be spending time with me. Besides, I'm pregnant and need to eat *now*," said Simone. Laura laughed.

After they finished eating breakfast, Simone said, "Thanks again Mom. I haven't had food like that in such a long time."

"I'm glad you liked it honey. By the way, I brought some cans of shortening so you can make biscuits after we go back to New York."

"That's wonderful, Mom you're an angel."

"Simone, are you going to tell me what's going on between you and Thomas? He didn't behave like a man who think you guys are broken up. Do you two love each other?"

"Yes, we love each other, but the problem is that we're not compatible. Thomas wants me to move in with him, but I refused without getting married first. *I'm* not going to tell him he should marry me—and I don't want anyone else to either. We had an argument last night and I confirmed our breakup; he didn't take it well, so you probably won't see him before you leave."

"Oh, I hope my big mouth didn't make things worse."

"Don't worry Mom, everything is settled now. Thomas knows we have to go on with separate lives."

Martin surfaced from his stupor in the afternoon. He loved lounging in Simone's zero-gravity chair so much that Simone had to chase him out of her studio. She didn't think her hungover brother dozing by her desk presented the professional image she wanted to portray to her clients. After she closed for the day, Martin brought up a conversation he'd had with Derrick.

"Simone, last night Derrick told me he has feelings for you, did you ever feel the same way? I think Derrick's a great guy."

"Derrick is a good guy. He would be great for someone else one day, but I'm not in love with him. We're just friends. I'm sorry that he developed feelings for me; until recently, I had no idea they were there," said Simone.

"Maybe it's something you can think about after the baby comes. Being right next door, he could help out a lot," her brother suggested.

CHAPTER TWENTY
THOMAS

Thomas looked up when the waiter came with their food, but he'd lost his appetite, so he just left money for the bill and walked out.

He was trying to sort out what had just happened, Thomas replayed Simone's words to himself as he walked down the street. She'd called him a bully who didn't respect who she was. He couldn't say for certain that her statement wasn't true.

He'd thought the baby would bring them back together. Before tonight, he'd had plans to do more things with Simone as a couple so that she could see they were meant to be together. But she already had plans, plans to move back to the U.S. without him. How could she be so cold? Thomas drove around aimlessly until he parked outside a pub. Once inside, he stayed until closing time.

****

Weeks passed. Thomas frequented the pub every evening, not knowing what else to do. Sometimes he would chat up a woman until he realized the women he found interest in looked like or reminded him of Simone; he didn't want meaningless relationships, but he couldn't move on—his heart wouldn't let him.

Simone sent text updates on the baby. That was it. She never asked about him or how his day was going. He really wanted to go to the sonogram appointment she'd told him about, but he knew he wouldn't be able to see her and just walk away afterwards. And though he was happy when she decided not to move back to New York, Thomas did not want Simone to remain Derrick's tenant. His imagination tortured him continuously. He thought of Derrick as an idiot; but that idiot was younger, in better shape, and lived next door to Simone. More importantly, Derrick was not an addict in recovery. The thought of Derrick becoming his son's stepfather made Thomas cringe. Would his son call Derrick "Daddy" one day?

After weeks of torturing himself with pubs and women, Thomas called the real estate agent he'd used to find his grandmother's cottage. He gave the agent Simone's contact details with instructions to find a building to house her studio and home. Thomas envisioned a nice home with a large backyard so his son would have space to play. He decided to send Simone a text.

"Hi Simone, sorry I couldn't make the sonogram appointment, something came up at the last minute. I was speaking to my real estate agent and I asked her about your need for more space once the baby arrives. Hope you don't mind my sending her over to you, she has several properties that she would like to show you."

Instead of a call thanking him for his thoughtfulness, Simone replied that she didn't want to move this late in the pregnancy.

A few days later, Thomas's mother showed up unannounced at his home to talk with him. The argument they had kept him in a bad mood. She asked if she could visit Simone and apologize, but Thomas told her that it wasn't a good time.

He didn't want to give Simone another reason to stay away from him.

CHAPTER TWENTY-ONE
SIMONE

Simone's father and Martin weren't happy about her decision not to move, but they understood that she didn't want to give up her business.

Derrick continued to stay clear of her on Friday mornings. She thought sometimes about how life would have been better for everyone if Derrick were the man she'd fallen in love with; but, as was her experience, love is messy and disappointing in the end. With the pregnancy hormones and the breakup with Thomas, Simone struggled to hide her sadness from her friends and family. Her days became routine; after finishing work Simone would eat dinner, take care of errands, watch some television, and go to sleep. Nikki and Becky called often to invite Simone to events or meals, but she would tell them she was tired just so she could stay at home by herself. Thomas not showing up for her six- and seven-month sonogram appointments made her think that he wasn't interested in the pregnancy and that he was only waiting for the end result.

The baby was growing well; Simone had gained eleven pounds since her hospital stay and at 33 weeks' gestation, she possessed a small basketball-like stomach that protruded high from her abdomen while the rest of her body, except for her chest, kept its normal petite size. Becky, noticing Simone's low moods, encouraged Simone to keep her spirits up. After she told Simone that wallowing in depression could hurt the baby and cause lower birth weight, Simone made a conscious effort to remain positive in spite of her situation. She created a habit of singing uplifting music in the morning and her son would sometimes kick in response.

When Simone was in the third and final trimester, the baby wasn't as active, and she wasn't sleeping well; her back would ache and her lungs felt compressed whenever she laid flat. For many nights, the zero-gravity chair Thomas brought was the only place she could fall asleep peacefully.

Being a sole proprietor meant she needed someone to run her business while she was out. Her plan was to stay away from direct customer contact for a minimum of six weeks, an average maternity leave period in the U.S. Simone devised a strategy where her mother would take one month off from her job to stay with the baby, and during that time she would ask Thomas to help with finding a good nanny. For those first six weeks, Simone's new trainee, Tracey, would open the studio and handle the customers until Simone was back at work. It was beneficial for her to live where she worked; if Tracey had a problem, Simone would be on hand to sort it out.

The mother-to-be felt beyond ready to give birth. She created a list to make sure nothing was left out. The crib and car seat were purchased. Her bag was packed. Tracey had keys to the shop and she knew to contact Derrick if she had any problems. Simone texted Thomas to make sure he had a baby car seat and crib on hand.

Back in New York, Simone's parents were getting along very well; her father was healthy, his transfer had come through, and he was back working in New York. Laura made Simone promise not to buy any baby clothes because she had purchased and shipped tons of baby clothing and layette items; she was looking forward to spoiling her only grandchild. Laura wanted to come for Simone's birthday and stay until the birth of her grandchild, but Simone insisted again that it would be better for her mother to save her vacation time for when the baby arrived.

On Simone's birthday, Nikki and Becky insisted Simone get out of the house; they found a spa that provided therapeutic back massages for pregnant women, and Becky reminded her that after the baby came, she wouldn't have much time to pamper herself. After the massage, her friends took Simone to a salon for a pedicure and hair conditioning treatment, and Simone truly enjoyed being taken care of by her friends. Even Derrick checked on her some mornings: he'd learned that ginger tea helped combat nausea, and he would show up with a mug every so often. Simone thought that was very sweet of him.

****

One evening, Simone sat in bed finishing up a client's design work on her laptop. It was after midnight when she decided to put her work away and change for bed. The phone rang just as she finished undressing. Simone sighed, thinking the call was from Martin, who frequently forgot about the time difference in England, but then Simone saw that her phone showed a London number she didn't recognize. "Hello, who is this calling?" she asked.

"Excuse me miss; I'm looking for someone who knows a Thomas Lloyd?"

"I know him, is there something I can help you with?"

"Yes miss, this is the bartender at The Mayors Pub on Tillery Lane in Richmond. We're closing up the pub now but the fellow here is in no shape to drive home. He gave me his phone to call someone. Your name had several stars next to it so I thought you might come and drive him home."

Simone sighed deeply and thought, *Not only did Thomas not come to any of the sonograms, now I have to pick him up from the pub after midnight—at eight months' pregnant.* "Yes I'll come, what is your address again?" After the bartender relayed the information, Simone angrily put her clothes back on and got in her car.

She arrived at the pub in little time because the streets were empty. Simone parked directly in front of the building; it was the only one around that still had light on inside. When she opened the door, the bartender looked down at her protruding belly.

"Oh, miss, you're in no condition to handle the likes of him," he stated.

"I'll tell you what, you put him in the back of my car and I'll handle the rest. If he doesn't wake up by the time I drive home, he'll just have to sleep in the car," said Simone. Seeing how angry she was made the bartender wish he'd called one of the un-starred numbers, but it was too late to do that now. The burly barkeep threw one of Thomas's arms around his neck, then half walked, half dragged Thomas to the back seat of Simone's car. After that, Simone reached home quickly and parked in front of her studio. She opened the back door and called Thomas to wake him up, but there was no movement. Simone poked him in the ribs, then slapped him on the cheek, but he didn't budge. "I don't have time for this," she said to herself.

Simone closed the door and went into the house with the intention of leaving Thomas in the back seat to sleep it off. Then she thought about all the neighbors walking by and seeing Thomas sleeping in her car. A new idea came to mind;

Simone went to the kitchen and filled a resealable plastic bag with ice. Banging the bag on the counter broke the ice into smaller pieces. Simone emptied the small pieces in a pitcher and mixed it with cold water. Back at the car, she unbuttoned Thomas's shirt and poured the ice water down his chest. He jumped in shock, nearly hitting his head on the roof of the car. Simone laughed so hard she had to hold her belly.

The now freezing-cold Thomas looked around, disoriented; he had no idea how he'd gotten into Simone's car. "Thomas, get up and come inside the house," said Simone. It wasn't a suggestion. Thomas clumsily exited the back seat and stood outside the car, still bewildered. He started looking around the street. "Thomas, what are you looking for?"

"You never know when Lemmings will pop up," he said drunkenly.

"Oh, I took care of Lemmings. You don't have to worry; he'll never bother you again." Thomas was confused by Simone's statement but he did as she asked.

Once inside she said, "You go in the bathroom and shower, I'll get you a robe and a sleep T-shirt since that's all I have that will fit you. Throw your clothes out when you're ready and I'll put them in the washing machine. You can sleep on the sofa bed."

Simone pulled out linen to use for the sofa; then she collected Thomas's clothes and placed them in the washer. He was still in the bathroom when she was finished, so she waited for him on the zero-gravity chair (which was now in her living room—Martin had brought it there so she could elevate her feet while watching television).

By the time Thomas walked out of the bathroom, more alert than before and feeling silly in the night shirt, Simone was fast asleep in the chair. He felt ashamed that she had had to take care of him in her condition. Thomas went to her bedroom, removed the blanket from her bed, and spread it over the sleeping Simone before he went to sleep on the sofa bed.

Thomas woke to the smells of ham and eggs; his stomach responded with a growl, and it reminded him that he had hardly eaten anything recently. Instead, he'd mostly been frequenting the pub since Simone left him at the restaurant. It wasn't a trendy pub; the regulars were local, middle-aged working-class men who had a beer or two after work. So far, no one had recognized him; he felt safe there.

Thomas heard a beautiful, sweet mezzo-soprano voice singing; he didn't recognize the song, but it was very calming and serene. "Ouch," he heard Simone say from the kitchen. Though his head was killing him, Thomas decided to get up to see if she needed help. As expected, he found Simone in the kitchen, her auburn hair in pigtails; with no makeup she looked like an innocent, freckle-face eighteen-year-old.

"Simone, are you alright?"

"Good morning, yes, I'm fine. That was your son kicking to let me know he doesn't like the song choice for this morning."

"Simone, I never knew you could sing. Your voice is beautiful," said Thomas.

"Thank you; sometimes I sing in the choir, I'm going to sing this song tomorrow. I started singing to the baby a month ago; sometimes it calms him down and he stops trying to kick his way out, other times, like now, it makes him more active. Do you want to feel them?" Thomas walked over to Simone and she placed his hand over her abdomen. The small thuds he felt made him smile.

"This is amazing, he's kicking so much."

"Welcome to my world," Simone said with a smile. "I have an idea, why don't you come to church with me tomorrow since it will be the last time I sing in the choir for a while. You can sit with Becky until I finish."

"I would love to see you sing. I'll be there."

"Great, I have to stay for both services so you can come during the second service. Are you ready for breakfast? I placed your clothes, towels, and a toothbrush by the couch."

"Thanks, I'll just go wash up and be back in a few minutes."

Thomas felt much better after taking a shower and some acetaminophen tablets. Simone kept the breakfast warm until he came back. She'd made country ham, spinach omelets, and American biscuits, unsure if Thomas had ever had American biscuits before since she hadn't yet found an equivalent to them in London. She watched Thomas pick one up and look at it strangely before she decided to help him out. She picked her biscuit up for reference and said, "These are what we call biscuits in America. I've searched but you have nothing like them in England, the closest bread is a scone. These are usually unsweetened and eaten with breakfast or fried chicken; give it a try. You could put butter or jam on it if you like." Thomas bit into one after putting butter on it.

"Hmm, I like it! It has a much softer texture than a scone."

"My mother brought a few containers of vegetable shortening over for me because I can't find our brand here, and it's one of the main ingredients." The two ate breakfast together, enjoying each other's company.

They were having pleasant conversation when Thomas decided to clear the air. "Simone, are you angry with me for the bartender calling you so late at night? I'm so sorry about that; I didn't think he would call you."

"Well, initially I was, since he called when I was going to bed; but I'm not angry anymore, I'm glad that you were smart enough to get a designated driver instead of attempting to drive while drunk. I don't mind doing it if it keeps you safe. But...why are you getting drunk? I never thought you would do something like that after going through rehab."

"You're right, I shouldn't be behaving this way; it's not a habit I should develop, and I'm not going to do it again. Thank you for coming to my rescue."

"You're welcome, but you didn't answer my question. Why are you getting drunk?" Simone asked again.

"I don't have an easy answer for that; I'm not sure why." Thomas got up and decided to change the subject. "How is your garden doing now?"

"Oh, it's much better. I raised the planting beds like you suggested. Let's take a look." They both walked through the French doors in her bedroom to view the garden.

"This looks great Simone, everything is doing remarkably well. Your rosemary seedlings are growing well. You must have done more than raise the planting beds," he said.

"I did add a special organic fertilizer to the soil," said Simone.

"That is some special fertilizer to get these results. By the way, when you said you 'took care of Lemmings,' exactly what did you mean?" Simone looked at Thomas, who had a smirk on his face.

"Thomas, you are terrible," she said as they both laughed at his joke. As they walked back into the house, Thomas noticed Simone seemed calmer with him; it was as if he no longer had any effect on her. He had a sudden urge to kiss her, but she'd made it clear that she wanted to move on, so he kept to himself. As they walked back to the kitchen, he decided it was time for him to confess to what he'd done—or, rather, hadn't done; there was nothing to lose at this point.

"Simone, I have to tell you something that I should have told you a long time ago." He didn't wait for her to reply, he had to tell her quickly or he'd lose his nerve. "On the night that we slept together, the first time I used a condom but I forgot to use one the second time. I didn't realize what I had done until afterwards."

Simone sighed. "Thomas, how could you forget something like that?"

"I'm so sorry Simone. I had every intention of using one. Please understand, I'd never made a mistake like that before, I've always protected myself." Simone sat sullenly, rubbing her belly. Thomas grabbed her hand. "Simone I'm sorry. Don't worry, I'll help with anything you want. I was thinking, I can pick the baby up every morning before you start work and he can spend his days with me. I know my grandmother will also help, and I will hire a nanny for you. You'll never feel burdened, and as soon as you're ready, I'll get you a bigger home." Simone stayed silent, deep in thought. "Simone, say something, I didn't mean to make you feel bad, I just wanted you to know the truth. I've been waiting for a good time to tell you but that time doesn't exist."

"It's alright Thomas, this is my fault too. I should have made sure you used one, or better yet, I shouldn't have had sex in the first place. I'm not supposed to, and I wasn't on birth control; I have to take responsibility for my own actions."

Still holding her hand, he said, "Don't take this the wrong way, I know neither of us planned to have this child, but I'm happy that you decided to have him." Simone looked away from his gaze so that he didn't see the tears coming down her cheeks. She stood up and walked away to her bedroom.

Thomas walked to the bedroom and knocked on the closed door. "Simone, what's wrong? I'm sorry if what I said upset you, that wasn't my intention. Can I come in?"

"No I'm fine. I'll see you at church tomorrow, OK?"

Thomas sighed. Just a few moments ago, he'd thought they were having a nice time together. But now, he could hear her crying and had no idea what to do, so Thomas collected his things and exited as she'd requested.

****

Simone woke up at noon and immediately regretted crying herself to sleep while Thomas was there. Everything had been fine until he'd held her hand and told her that he was happy she was having his baby. She wanted more from him, but Thomas had made it clear that he only wanted her to move in with him. Co-parenting was going to be harder than she realized; however, there was nothing she could do to change the circumstances. Thomas was a well-known celebrity who could only see himself marrying a woman like his former girlfriend Judy, not a woman of faith like herself. Still, she had to apologize; Thomas was most likely dumbfounded at her crying, and she didn't want him to use her fluctuating emotions as an excuse to back out of attending church services, so she sent him a text.

"Hi Thomas, I'm sorry about this morning. I was being overly emotional. These pregnancy hormones can be embarrassing at times. I'm looking forward to seeing you tomorrow. I shared Becky's cell phone number with you and I've texted her your number. Becky will call you when she's seated, and will save a seat for you."

CHAPTER TWENTY-TWO
CHURCH SERVICES

As Thomas drove to Simone's church the next morning, he mulled over the argument they'd had in the restaurant weeks ago. Thomas realized then that what Simone had said was true. He did want her to live his way; it was the only way he was used to, and the women in his past had never had an issue with it. But he understood that he was wrong for wanting to change her, and he hoped that attending Simone's church would help her see that he loved her just the way she was.

Yes, she was a pretty woman, but that beauty wasn't what had held his attention in the car after she'd rescued him and Alistair. It was her character and values. Simone had dignity; she wasn't like the other women he'd been with, and nothing like his mother had accused her of being. Those other women would have sent their lawyers to him, demanded a huge monthly payout for them and the child. Those were the women who would quickly jump into his bed, not caring if he knew their name. No, his fame and money didn't dazzle Simone; she'd been willing to walk away with nothing after his mother made that repulsive offer. She didn't need or depend on him, but their child had created a bond between them that prevented her from writing him off completely, and he was grateful for that.

This invitation to watch her sing gave Thomas hope; he saw it as an olive branch, but he knew he couldn't allow his hopes to get too high. The invite into her life could be solely for their child's sake. He felt awkward going alone, so he'd called his grandmother to accompany him for support; and thinking of their phone conversation made him laugh to himself. She'd turned up her hearing aid to make certain she'd heard him correctly.

"What's that you said? You're going to church and you want me to come with you?" she'd asked in disbelief.

"Yes Gran, that's what I said. Will you be ready by 9 AM?"

"Yes, yes, I will be ready, sweetheart!"

Thomas imagined his gran with her hands clasped together, looking to the heavens and saying, *"Thank You Father,"* after hanging up the phone.

They arrived at the busy church parking lot just after the first service ended. Thomas waited in his Land Rover with his grandmother until the bulk of exiting traffic cleared the lot.

Meanwhile, inside the church, some members lingered in prayer around the altar. Simone was relaxed and content; singing gospel songs always left her in a joy-filled mood. As she walked off stage with the choir, she searched the seats and wondered if Thomas would actually show up. Becky spotted her first and waved Simone over. They greeted each other with a hug before sitting.

"Thomas told me to save him two seats, he's bringing an extra person," said Becky.

"I wonder who?" said Simone.

"We'll soon find out; I'm going to search for them now," said Becky as she left her seat. The second-session congregants were filing into the church while Becky waited to exit. Outside the entrance, Becky stood away from the crowd and shielded her eyes from the sun as she searched for Thomas. Just then, her phone received a text.

"Hi Becky, we're here. I can see where you're standing so don't move, we'll be there in a few minutes." Becky spotted Thomas walking across the parking lot with an elderly woman who used a cane. "Hello again Becky, it's good to see you. This is my grandmother. Gran, Becky is a close friend of Simone's."

"It's nice to meet you, Mrs. Lloyd," said Becky.

"It's a pleasure to meet you too, dear. My, you have a very large church."

"Yes, we've been growing in attendees every year. We have approximately 1,400 members to date," said Becky as she escorted them to the main level seats where Simone was waiting. When Simone saw Mrs. Lloyd, she stood up and gave her a hug and kiss before saying hello to Thomas. They all sat together and talked until Simone had to leave to rejoin the choir on stage. Thomas took a look around; the congregation was quite large, with young and old mixed together. With his experience singing in different arenas, he estimated the current congregation to be approximately 500 people—and this was the second service of the day. He'd never been in a church of this size. Thomas received a few curious glances from some congregants, but thankfully no one approached him for an autograph.

As the musicians began playing the intro to a song he'd never heard before, the congregation stood up. There were screens above the stage displaying the lyrics to the songs so that the those assembled could sing along. This wasn't how Thomas remembered services in his grandmother's church.

The first song was called "The Anthem." The male soloist who sung it had very powerful vocals, and Simone sang the chorus along with the other choir members. The congregants were swaying and waving their hands to the music; some closed their eyes and whispered prayers. The next song was "Oceans," the one he'd heard Simone singing to their child yesterday. Thomas thought Simone's solo was beautiful; he was very impressed with her voice. Looking at the lyrics on the screen, he now believed he understood its meaning. From what he could remember from when he'd attended church with his grandmother as a child, the song was about Peter walking on water. When Peter focused on Jesus, he walked on water, when he lost his faith temporarily, he began to sink until he cried out to Jesus, who saved him. Thomas wondered if Simone had picked this song because she identified with it.

The choir sang another song, then exited the stage before the pastor came to the pulpit. A few minutes later, Simone arrived and sat next to Thomas.

Before he could say anything, his grandmother reached over him and whispered to Simone, "That was a lovely song, dear." Simone held her hand and thanked her. In that moment, Thomas realized how similar the two women were: both had strong morals and good character; neither allowed money or circumstances to change who they were; and they both lived by their faith. He was glad he'd come to church today. Being there and listening to the conversations she had with his grandmother revealed more of who Simone was, and he loved her even more.

But then his grandmother started a new conversation with Simone. "And how is the young man who gave up his seat for me?"

"Oh, you mean my friend Derrick. He's fine, sometimes he brings me ginger tea in the mornings because he read that it helps with nausea," said Simone.

"Isn't that so thoughtful of him, he is a very good friend," said his grandmother. Thomas rolled his eyes; he was tired of hearing about Simone's landlord, and he was certain Derrick wasn't bringing tea to any of his other tenants in the morning.

Then the pastor asked everyone to take out their Bibles. Simone took out her tablet and opened her Bible app. The pastor began, "Good morning, for today's sermon, we will continue with the question: Does God make bad things happen to us? Last week, we defined 'bad things' as disease, accidents, tragedies, and the like. We discussed chapter 1 in Genesis, where God made the earth with everything in it and said it was very good. We've also established that sin was not in the world at this time.

"Let's pick up from there; we know that God created the world without sin. What is sin? Sin is everything that is bad according to God's laws. We also know that Lucifer introduced sin into the world by tricking Eve, who then gave the forbidden fruit to Adam. Romans 5:12 explains this, "'Wherefore, as by one man sin entered into the world, and death by sin; and so, death passed upon all men, for that all have sinned.'

"Now, there are many descriptions of sin in the Bible; for the sake of time, I'll read one list. In 2 Timothy 3:2-5, the Bible states: 'For people will be lovers of self, lovers of money, proud, arrogant, abusive, disobedient to their parents, ungrateful, unholy, heartless, unappeasable, slanderous, without self-control, brutal, not loving good, treacherous, reckless, swollen with conceit, lovers of pleasure rather than lovers of God, having the appearance of godliness, but denying its power.'

"Let's discuss bad things. What happens when a tornado destroys a house? The insurance company calls it an 'act of God.' When people die from illness, murder, or an accident, some say, 'God needed another angel.' These statements are not just untrue; they are bold lies. Don't believe me? Read the Bible for yourself! Where in it does God say your illness, murder, or accident was performed by Him? You can look all you want, read between the lines, but you will never find this. God is our Father, our parent; there are many places in the Bible that state this, but I like 2 Corinthians 6:18 the best. It says, 'I will be a Father to you, and you will be my sons and daughters, says the Lord Almighty.'"

"Do you know of any parent who wants to see their child suffer from illness, be murdered, or die in a terrible accident? Of course not, a parent wants to protect their child from the ills and dangers of this world. They will say things like, 'Johnny, don't stick your hand in the fire; if you do, you will get burned.' Or they may say, 'Don't run into the street; if you do, a car may hit and kill you.' Can Johnny still stick his hand in the fire and run into the street? Yes, he can do these things and suffer the consequences, but it's not the parent who burns the child or runs him over. Why would a parent go through all the trouble of creating the child just to torture and kill him? Also, would a parent do these things while saying, 'love your neighbor and help one another'?

"Who might you say is responsible for these things, if God, our parent, is not? Now that's a good question. I want you to turn to 1 John 5:19. It says, 'We know that we are from God, and the whole world lies in the power of the evil one.' Who is the evil one? The same one who tricked Eve and Adam into bringing sin into the world. He's called Lucifer, Beelzebub, Satan; these are some of his names. He is the evil one, it is he who wants to destroy man. Now let's read 1 John 10:10. Jesus says, 'The thief only comes to steal and kill and destroy. I came that they may have life and may have it abundantly.' Now who do you think Jesus is referring to in this verse? One thing we do know is that the thief wants to harm us, or take something valuable from us. Now here's a question for those of you who believe God controls all and everything in this world. Why would God warn us to watch out for the thief who steals, kill, and destroys if he's the one doing the stealing, killing, and destroying?" The pastor continued reviewing the passage until he finished the sermon.

"Next week we'll recap this discussion before moving on to free will and the choice to sin. At this time, I would like the choir to return and lead us into song. As they sing, if anyone is ready to give themselves to Christ and have their sins forgiven so they will no longer be spiritually dead, please come forward to the altar."

Before Simone stood to join the other choir members who were returning to the stage, she left her tablet and handbag with Thomas, who was reading the rest of the book of John on his own. She was surprised by how intently he'd been listening to the pastor.

Both the pastor and prayer team members prayed for the people who approached the altar while Simone and the other choir members sang "The Anthem" again, the congregation singing along. When they finished, the pastor dismissed the church and people began exiting the building. Some of the choir members were hugging Simone goodbye before she came back to her seat.

"I'm sorry it took a little longer for me to get here," said Simone when she returned to her friends.

"That's alright dear, it's good to keep in touch with your friends," said Mrs. Lloyd.

Becky stood up. "Well, I'll be on my way. It was nice to meet you, Mrs. Lloyd. Thomas, it was good to see you again. Simone, you did a lot today, make sure you get rest; I will call you tomorrow," said Becky.

"Thanks for your help Becky," said Simone. Thomas and his grandmother also said goodbye to Becky, then Thomas turned to Simone and asked, "Simone, why don't you come with me and Gran to lunch?"

"That sounds nice, but I'm too tired to eat right now. I was here hours before the first service to rehearse. Now I just want to take a nap."

"Dear, you need your rest but you can't skip meals. Thomas, why don't we go to lunch and then bring food over to Simone. That way she can rest first," said Mrs. Lloyd.

"Sounds good to me, is that fine with you?" asked Thomas.

"That's perfect. I'll see you two later," said Simone.

CHAPTER TWENTY-THREE
MRS. LLOYD

These young people have very different ways of living; everything has changed since my days. I do try to stay out of my grandson's personal business because that's how he likes it, and I have no intention of being like his mum. He is a grown man who doesn't need anyone meddling in his life, but I'm 84 years old, and I want to see my Thom happy before I leave.

He did good when he gave up the drugs. I'm so proud of him for staying clean; and he's accomplished so much. A genius on the keyboards, a music composer; Thomas has done very well for himself. He knows how to run his music business and I'm delighted with his success.

But he can be daft! Oh, I just want to shake him sometimes; what a hard-headed boy. Take Judy for instance; she wasn't for him. I heard that one had an eye for every man who walked in the room. Thom's mother did him a favor, that she did. Marrying Judy would have been a major disaster, and it would have been his disaster to fix.

I did not get involved in that mess, but I've held my tongue about the Simone situation for too long. I'd hoped Thom would've figured it out on his own, but he hasn't made the right move.

Something has to be said because it's breaking my heart to see those two separated when it's obvious they belong together.

Oh, look at my poor Thom, he's so distressed he hasn't touched his food.

"Thomas, you look troubled. Are you thinking of Simone?"

"Gran, I don't know what to do. I want to be with her, especially during this time in her pregnancy. She's all alone right now. Her mother was to come this week but Simone told her to come closer to the due date. It's not a good situation; if she falls again there's no one there to see anything. I'm worried about her."

"Thomas, what is the problem between you two? You love Simone, and I can tell by the way she looks at you that she loves you too. Both of you created a baby that will be here in a few weeks. Why don't you just go ahead and ask her to marry you?"

"Gran, you know my history; I'm an addict in recovery. Simone knows about everything I did in the past, and she recently had to drive me home when I was drunk. A woman like Simone could never see herself married to the likes of me. I'm just hoping she'll get used to me being around so much, because of the baby, and she'll realize I'm not the worthless screw-up I used to be; that she'll see that I'm changed. But if I ask her now, I know she'll turn me down, and I won't be able to handle it."

"Why do you think she will say no?"

"Gran, I asked Simone to move in with me several time. I've given her the keys to my house. Instead of smiling, she looked sad, and said we couldn't be together. Thanks to the media, she knows about all the vile and shameful things I've done."

Mrs. Lloyd shook her head. "Thom, if your grandfather had asked me to move in with him, he would have had the keys thrown back in his face. Listen, you told me she ended the relationship because she didn't want to have premarital sex. Don't you realize that asking her to move in with you was an insult? That's why the poor dear was sad. And as far as your background goes, am I correct in assuming she continued to go with you even after she knew what sort of past you had? If it wasn't an issue then, it shouldn't be one now; especially since you've created a child with her; besides, you are nothing like you were back then.

"I'll tell you one thing: I like Simone. So, if you don't have the guts to ask her to marry you, you should step aside. When I visited her in the hospital, I overheard that nice gentleman, Derrick, telling Simone that he loves her. He seems like a sweet young man, and they would make a nice couple. Hmm, I wonder if she would allow me to attend their wedding?"

"Grandmother, what are you saying? Would you really go to a wedding that breaks my heart?"

"I would if you don't have the sense to go after her before you lose the woman you love. You know what your problem is? You've been spoiled by your money, and the women you've shagged. You've never had to work for your relationships because they all came to you without any effort. Now that you have someone who truly loves you, you're backing away because keeping the relationship requires work, work you never had to do in your past. Thom, how are you going to feel if Derrick asks her to marry him first? She might say no now; but over time, she may warm up to the idea."

Thomas sighed. "Gran, you're being cruel; where is all of this coming from?"

Mrs. Lloyd grabbed Thomas's hands, "It's coming from my heart Thom. I've watched the two of you together, you enjoy each other's company. Don't go through the rest of your life wondering "what if?" If you want something, go for it. If she says no, it will hurt terribly, but then there's no regret."

Thinking about all his grandmother had just said, Thomas

began to nod in agreement. "Gran, you are right; I'm going to ask her. I'll do whatever it takes."

"That's my boy!" she said, still grasping his hands.

"Gran, can I borrow this ring on your finger?" Thomas started pulling at the ring.

"Wait, Thom, what are you going to do with my ring?"

"There's not enough time for me to buy one before I go back to Simone's. I'm going to propose to her today; I'll use your ring for now, and I'll let her pick her own later. That is, if she says yes."

"That's wonderful, Thom; I'm so happy now. Yes, you can use the ring. I can't wait to see her face!"

"Um, Gran...I'm going to drop you home first; this is something I must do on my own."

"Well, alright, I understand son," she said dejectedly.

They left the restaurant with Simone's lunch and Thomas dropped his grandmother off at his house where he stopped quickly to grab his keyboard and a lyric sheet. After a few minutes of thinking, Thomas wrote down words from his heart before speeding off to Simone.

Filled with anxiety at the thought of Simone turning his proposal down, Thomas gripped the steering wheel as he headed for her home.

She came quickly to the door when he rang. "Hi Thomas, come in; that was a long lunch. My stomach began growling, then Jethro started kicking, so I cheated and ate some grapes. Wait, where's your grandmother?"

"Um, she's had a great deal of excitement today, so she's resting at my place for a bit. Did you say 'Jethro'? Please tell me that's not the name you picked for our son."

"What's wrong with Jethro? It's a name taken from the Bible, just like the name Thomas," stated Simone. She spotted a cake container in the food items that Thomas had brought and reached out for it.

"Oh no, you must eat your lunch first before dessert."

"Thomas, I'm a hungry pregnant woman, I can eat my cake first!"

"No, I won't allow it, you have to think of your blood sugar," he said, hoping she'd relent. "Save the dessert for last."

"Well, OK, I guess you're right."

"You sit down and I'll warm up the food for you."

"Hey, what's the keyboard for?"

"Um, I'm working on a new song, and I wanted to see what you thought about it."

"Oh Thomas, I'm honored that you want my opinion. I'm looking forward to hearing it," said Simone.

****

"Thanks for lunch, Thomas, I loved the salmon." Simone started to stand up but Thomas stopped her.

"Wait. Stay there, I'll bring your dessert and you can hear the song at the same time." Thomas quickly removed the dish and retrieved the cake container from the refrigerator. He took out the dessert, a puffed pastry with whipped cream and fresh assorted berries on top, and placed the ring over the center berry. Thomas plugged in his keyboard and placed it on a chair before setting the dessert container in front of Simone.

Simone looked at the dessert. She saw the ring and looked at Thomas with a confused expression. Then Thomas went down on one knee and played the keyboard while he sang.

FOR THE LOVE OF SIMONE
You rescued me out of the night
I saw you then in the dark light

Green, the color of your sexy eyes
Your gaze broke the mask from my guise

Simone, I'm down on my knees
Beggin' you to love me please
To your heart, I'll always sing
Please say yes and take this ring

Remember our night in the park?
Was it then that you opened your heart?
Stars in your eyes when I held your hand
Wondered am I part of her plan?

Simone, I'm down on my knees
Beggin' you to love me please
To your heart, I'll always sing
Please say yes and take this ring

She gathered me in her arms, I took it as a sign
What can I do if you won't be mine?
Broken hearted, spirit darkened, and I lost my way
Tried so many ways to hold you, baby please stay

Simone, I'm down on my knees
Beggin' you to love me please
To your heart, I'll always sing
Please say yes and take this ring

Tears rolled down Simone's face after the first chorus. By the end of the song, she covered her face with her hands and cried profusely. Thomas believed her tears were a good sign but he needed to be certain. "You're crying, does this mean the answer is yes?" Simone nodded yes, stood up, and put her arms around him. Relieved, Thomas held her for several minutes while she cried.

Then Simone stopped and pulled back abruptly. "Please tell me you're not marrying me only because I'm pregnant?"

"Simone, you have no idea how much I love you; of course it's not just because you're pregnant. I've wanted you in my life for a long time, but I know I'm not your ideal choice for a partner. I convinced myself that you'd never marry a recovering addict. I want you to know that I keep up with all my therapy sessions, and you're welcome to attend any of them."

"Thomas, you are my ideal choice, because I love you; and I love that you revealed everything about your past when we first met. I would never hold that against you."

"Simone, let's get married right away. I'm thinking tomorrow!"

"Tomorrow?! How can we do it so soon? Maybe we should wait until after we have the baby. That way I can fit into a proper dress."

"No, that's too long. We can have a ceremony after the baby but I want you living with me before then, and I was thinking it would be better for us to marry before the baby comes. We could get married on Friday?"

"But my mom's coming this Saturday. I know, we can get married next Sunday."

"Simone, that's a whole week."

"Yes, but it will give us a little time to plan something."

"Well, if that's what you want, but you're living with me from next Sunday on. In fact, I'll send someone over during the week to help you pack, because I don't want you to lifting anything."

"There's so much to do, I don't know where to start."

"Don't worry, we'll have a small ceremony at my house. I'll take care of the planning, all you'll have to do is show up. I'll leave now to make some calls, but give me a kiss for the road." Delighted, Simone gave Thomas a passionate goodbye kiss.

"Hmmm, you're kissing much better now for some reason. You've been holding back on me," teased Thomas.

"My kisses are better because I'm happy," Simone said with a smile.

"I'd better leave now then. Oh, before I forget, I'm taking you to the jeweler tomorrow to get a proper ring. This one's a loaner from Gran."

"Tell her thank you for me!"

"I will, I'm sure she's waiting by the phone right now for my call."

****

Overjoyed, Simone called everyone she knew, starting with Nikki. "Nikki, I need your help with something. Will you have an afternoon off to go shopping with me this week?"

"Simone, is this really you? You're asking *me* to go shopping? You're the same woman I had to drag kicking and screaming to the shops. What's the occasion? You know, they have some really sexy maternity clothing now."

"Well, Thomas's invited me to a special event next Sunday. By the way, you're invited too; can you make it?"

"Yes, I can make it, but what's the occasion?"

"Invitations are not ready yet, but they will say, "You are cordially invited to attend the wedding of Miss Simone Mills and Mr. Thomas Lloyd!"

"Oh my goodness, Simone, are you serious!"

"Yes, very much so."

"Tell me what happened?"

"Thomas brought my lunch and dessert. When he gave me the dessert, he had a wedding ring on top! Then, he got down on his knee and sang his proposal to me while playing his keyboard. In the chorus he asked me to take his ring."

"Simone that's wonderful, I'm so happy for you! I can't wait; I'm going to search online right now for the perfect dress and send you the links."

Simone called her mother and father next. They were very happy at the news; her father made plans to fly out on Saturday with her mother, and they promised to fill Martin in. She called Becky after that, who was also so happy for Simone and promised to be there for the ceremony.

Simone had so many things to think of. She pulled out her trunk and started packing clothing and toiletries she would need once she moved into Thomas's house.

****

On Monday afternoon, Thomas took Simone to Hatton Garden to pick out the perfect ring. She'd hardly gotten any sleep the night before because it had felt like the baby was laying on her lungs. Looking for the ring wore her out, but together they chose the perfect set of platinum wedding bands. The next day, Nikki took her to two shops that sold maternity wedding gowns, and the women picked out the ideal champagne-colored empire-waist chiffon dress. To meet the wedding date deadline, the shop expedited the alterations needed to fit Simone's petite body, promising to have it ready on Thursday morning; Nikki made arrangements to go with Simone to pick up the dress and matching shoes.

Meanwhile, Libby arranged for a wedding planner to come decorate the great room in Thomas's house. After that she had a to-do list that included booking a caterer, a bakery for the cake, and a florist. Thomas asked his grandmother to find them a pastor who could marry them quickly, and she found an Anglican priest who reluctantly agreed to perform the quickie ceremony after she told him of the impending birth.

Thomas was busy preparing as well. He called his family, Alistair, and the rest of the band members, ensuring everyone would attend. He spoke with his fiancée several times a day to keep her up to date with the plans. Simone wanted to get more involved with the planning, but Thomas advised against it; with the baby due in three and a half weeks, Simone had become increasingly more fatigued. Thomas could see it in her eyes when they did meet.

On Thursday, Nikki took the day off to spend with Simone. Nikki was secretly planning a hen night for Saturday evening so that Simone's mother could attend. During the day, Nikki took Simone to the salon to find a hairstyle for Simone's long, thick, auburn hair that would go well with the style of her chiffon dress; they settled on a modern updo with tendrils on one side of her face and a floral rhinestone brooch. The women continued to the bridal shop; and with the professional alterations, Simone's dress fitted exceptionally well.

Back in the car, Nikki reviewed the photos taken in the dress shop. "You're looking very sexy for an eight-months-pregnant woman. I'll save these to add to the wedding photo album. Well that's it, everything is covered on your list. What do you say to lunch before I take you home?" Nikki waited for a response from her friend, but there was none. "Is something wrong? Aren't you excited?"

"I am, it's just that I'm very tired; I haven't been able to sleep much for the past few nights. Even though the baby hasn't been kicking as much, I can't seem to find a comfortable sleep position, and my backache never goes away."

"You poor thing, I can't imagine what you're going through; this baby has taken over your body. You're going to the bathroom every half hour, can't sleep, and you have to watch what you eat; but you've got to hang in there; it's just a few more weeks," said Nikki.

"Nikki, can we skip lunch? I just need to lie down right now," said Simone.

"Well, why don't you wait in the car while I grab some lunch to go, that way you can get off of your feet."

"Thanks Nikki, that sounds great, I just need to lie down for a few minutes." Simone pushed the passenger seat back as far as it would go and lay down. Eyes closed, she felt herself drifting toward sleep. After a few minutes, she experienced a sharp cramp that jolted her upright. It went away after a few seconds so she laid down again. When Nikki came back to the car, Simone was fast asleep, so Nikki decided to drive her home without waking her up. They arrived at Simone's home in ten minutes, and Simone rolled onto her side before sitting up.

"Now I feel rested; guess I really needed that nap. Thanks Nikki."

"Anything for the mother of my Godson. By the way, if you two haven't decided on a name yet, would you consider 'Nicholas?'" she said with a smirk.

"Hmmm, I wonder why you would pick that name, Nikki?"

"Well, I just thought it sounded like a good English name."

"Don't forget, this baby is half American," said Simone.

"That's not going to matter, he will be a British citizen when he's born here."

"You know, I never thought of that until you mentioned it; I'll have to find out how he can have dual citizenship."

Inside, the two women had just sat down to eat their lunches when Simone was seized with another sharp cramp that made her hold her abdomen. "Oh no, not now, this can't be happening now!"

"Simone, what's wrong!"

"I—I think I'm in labor, this is the second cramp today but it's three weeks too early!"

"You'd better call the doctor, maybe it's those pre-labor pain things."

Simone dialed the doctor's office. After speaking with the nurse, she turned to Nikki and said, "They put me on hold, they're waiting for the doctor to pick up the phone. I need to let Thomas know what's going on."

"Don't worry, I'll send him a text," said Nikki.

"Hi Thomas, it may be nothing but Simone might be having some contractions, she's on the phone to the doctor now. Will keep you posted."

Simone finished with the phone call and turned to Nikki. "The doctor wants me to come in so she can check me out, just in case. Nikki, I can't have the baby now. My mother's not here and the wedding is Sunday!"

"Don't worry, Simone, it's probably nothing; let's just get you to the doctor so she can check you out."

CHAPTER TWENTY-FOUR
THE WEDDING

They were caught in traffic on the way to the hospital when Simone had another contraction. It had been approximately 20 minutes since the last one. When they arrived, the hospital staff took her into the maternity ward where her cervix was checked, and they found that she was dilated four centimeters. A technician entered Simone's room and performed a sonogram. When Simone asked how the baby was, the technician told her the doctor would be in shortly to talk to her. Thomas arrived after the technician left.

"Simone, how are you feeling?" he said after he'd kissed her hello.

"I'm feeling like I should have listened to you and gotten married the day after you proposed. I'm sorry Thomas, it doesn't look like I'm going to make it to Sunday."

"Don't worry about that, just focus on the baby. What did the doctor say?"

"We're waiting for her to tell us what's next."

"Nikki, thanks for the text," he said.

"No problem. Um, I'm going to get a cup of coffee or something, I'll be back later."

Thomas peered at Simone's anxious expression and squeezed her hand. "Are you still worried about the wedding?"

"No, it's not that. I don't like the fact that the technician wouldn't look me in the eye after she did the exam. I'm worried about the baby."

"Simone, please try to relax; I'm sure worrying will only make you feel worse."

"You're right, I'm probably overreacting. I wish I'd let my mom come when she wanted to, she would have been with me today."

Before Thomas could respond, Doctor Rodsmith came into the room and closed the door. "Hello Simone, how are you feeling?"

"I'm feeling fine now. The contractions are twelve minutes apart. This is the baby's father, Thomas."

"Hello... Oh, you're Thomas Lloyd, aren't you?! It's good to meet you, and it's good that you are here," said the doctor as she shook his hand. "Now, I have some news but it's nothing to worry about. The baby is ready ahead of schedule. He's in the right position for birthing and your cervix has started dilating, but the baby's head is a bit large. We are going to continue monitoring the condition of your cervix."

"Does this mean I may need cesarean surgery?" asked Simone.

"There is a good chance that we'll have to perform a cesarean section because your birth canal may not be large enough for the baby's head to pass through. Try not to worry, I will come again in about an hour to check your status."

Thomas felt Simone's hand tense when the doctor mentioned surgery. "Simone don't stress about cesarean surgery, my sister-in-law had cesareans for all three of her kids; the procedure is very common, you will be fine."

"It's hard not to worry about it, I never thought about

surgery. I also wished I'd listened to you and gotten married when you asked; especially now when I'm set to move in with you with the baby," Simone said sadly.

Thomas thought of an idea. He kissed the top of her head and said, "I'll be right back." Glancing at the clock before leaving the room, Thomas noted the time was 3:03 PM; he'd have to act quickly if his plan was to work.

Watching Thomas sprint out the door, Simone grimaced as another contraction hit. Her mind wondered about all the things that could go wrong during a cesarean; she also worried about Thomas not being present when the baby was being born. *"Maybe this was too much drama for him to handle,"* she said to herself. Tired and alone, Simone closed her eyes to nap, but the worrying and contractions kept her from rest.

Some time passed before Becky and Nikki entered the hospital room together. Thomas had texted them about the possibility of Simone having surgery.

"Simone, cesarean births are so commonplace now," Becky assured her.

"Yeah, don't some celebrities schedule cesarean births to have control over their delivery times?" said Nikki.

"I know all of that, but I can't get rid of my fear," said Simone.

"Why don't we pray about it then," said Becky. While holding Simone's hand, she reached for Nikki's hand while Nikki grabbed Simone's other hand.

"Dear Lord,

"You told us to fear not. We ask that You help our sister Simone lose her fear. Give her confidence in her spirit to know that both she and her child will get through this birth successfully. Let them both be healthy and well after the delivery. We ask this in Jesus's name. Amen!"

"Thanks Becky, that was a nice prayer," said Simone.

"I liked that too; I didn't know you can pray about things like fear," said Nikki.

"You can pray for anything you want as long as it doesn't go against what God has already told us. Call me anytime if you want me to pray for you," said Becky.

"I may take you up on that offer one day," said Nikki. The friends stayed and talked with Simone about anything they could think of that would take her mind off her situation until the doctor returned to examine Simone. It wasn't long before the doctor confirmed that cesarean surgery was required.

Thomas rushed backed to Simone's room as the doctor left, completely out of breath, to find Nikki and Becky seated outside the door. "Hi ladies, it's good that you're both still here; I need you two to stay a little longer." As he finished, a stern-faced, elderly Anglican priest walked up to Thomas expectantly. Thomas ushered all parties into Simone's room.

"Thomas, what's wrong, why are you out of breath?" asked Simone.

"Simone, this is Father Kendrick; Father, this is my fiancée. I'm very sorry to rush you Father, but as you can see, we're pressed for time." As if on cue, Simone had another contraction; this time her water broke.

"Yes, yes, I see young man; we should start now!" said the flustered priest.

The ceremony went as quickly as the elderly priest could perform it. He made Becky and Nikki sign the registrar as witnesses after obtaining Simone's and Thomas's signatures. Simone thanked the priest before Thomas ushered him out to his driver's car.

"Simone I'm so happy for you, Thomas is a very caring husband," said Becky.

"I can't believe what just happed, I'll be calling you Mrs.

Lloyd from now on; I'm extremely happy for you too," gushed Nikki.

When Thomas returned, Becky and Nikki exited the room to give the newlyweds privacy. "Thomas, I can't believe you did that for me," said a tearful Simone.

"I did it for us, Mrs. Lloyd. Now I can kiss you anytime I want." Thomas leaned over and gave Simone a passionate kiss until she gasped in pain.

"Please tell Dr Rodsmith to come back now," she said. Thomas ran out of the room to find the doctor. Becky and Nikki came back in to comfort Simone while she writhed through the strongest contraction yet.

The doctor returned with an orderly and, together, they whisked Simone away to the birthing room. A nurse returned for Thomas. "Mr. Lloyd, please come with me, I will suit you up." Thomas followed closely behind the fast-walking nurse.

In the operating room, the nurses got Thomas into a gown and turned him around to face Simone, instructing him to keep her calm. A sheet was raised over her chest to prevent her and Thomas from seeing the surgery. Thomas was afraid for Simone but he didn't want to show it. He reached for her hand and said, "Just look at me, everything will be fine." They held hands while the doctor and staff worked, and Thomas could feel the tremble in Simone's hand.

"I'm so cold," she whispered.

"That's normal, the IV you're hooked up to is making you feel cold," said one of the nurses.

"I feel strange, what's happening now?" asked Simone as she tried to see what the doctor was doing.

The nurse watched Simone's expression before saying, "Please stay calm, the doctor is performing the procedure." The same nurse then whispered to Thomas, "Try to keep her attention away from the surgery." Thomas couldn't think of what to do. He knew his brother had gone through this with Sarah three times, but Thomas had never asked how he'd dealt with it. Sensing Simone's anxiety, he came up with a quick solution: he knelt down next to her face and started singing the ballad he'd sung to her at the concert. That did it; Simone gave him her full attention.

"Thom, you're singing that song now?" she asked with a smile. Thomas tried his best to sing quietly, but the operating room staff still heard him.

"Oh, that's so sweet," he heard one of the nurses say.

Simone was crying happy tears. "Thomas, I love you so much," she said.

He whispered in her ear, "I still can't wait to hear you shout, 'Thomas, I love you' all night long."

Simone laughed and whispered, "Are you trying to make me blush during my cesarean?"

The sound of their son crying filled the room before he could reply. The nurses cleaned and weighed the baby before bringing him his parents.

"Your baby's weight is six pounds and two ounces," said the nurse. Thomas was amazed by the whole experience. Simone began talking to their infant while the doctor completed the surgery. Simone saw tears in her husband's eyes when they smiled at each other over the baby's head.

Thomas was then escorted back to Simone's room. Elated, he called his brother and grandmother, who couldn't believe he'd gotten married and become a father in the same day.

James said, "You lucky dog, you'll never have to worry about forgetting your wedding anniversary; you only have to remember your son's birthday." Thomas's family wanted to come to the hospital that night, but the new father said it'd been a very long day for his family; tomorrow would be better.

Soon after he hung up the phone, the medical staff returned

Simone and their newborn to their room. Thomas held his baby boy for the first time and was unexpectedly overwhelmed with the love he felt for his son. With his child in his arms, Thomas leaned over the bed and kissed Simone.

"Thomas, how can you kiss me now? I know I'm not a pretty sight and I'll be starting our marriage with a huge scar."

"Simone, how can I not kiss you? You just went through hell to have our child and"—he placed his lips to her ear—"I can't wait to kiss your scar." Thomas laughed, "Wow, *now* you're blushing!" Laughing along, Simone reached out to hold their infant's hand. The new parents stayed like this for some time, quietly admiring their sleeping child.

Abruptly, Simone looked at Thomas and said, "Kendrick."

Confused, Thomas looked at Simone's expression, then he looked at their child. Nodding in agreement he said, "Yes, Kendrick from Father Kendrick; that's a good name."

"What about his middle name?" asked Simone.

"What do you think of Morden?"

"Yes, from Morden Hall Park where we watched the stars."

"Kendrick Morden Lloyd. Now that's a proper name for our son," said Thomas.

CHAPTER TWENTY-FIVE
FAMILY

Libby, Laura, and Thomas's mother arrived on the island early to set up arrangements for the couple's nuptials. Together, they'd coordinated every aspect of the ceremony.

The couple chose November 25 TH to renew their vows and have the reception that they'd previously had to cancel after Kendrick's early arrival.

That day, guests gathered around the barefoot couple as Simone and Thomas spoke their vows on the beach. Warm Bermuda breezes perfumed by the abundant floral shrubs were a sharp contrast to the chilled, damp weather they'd left behind in London. The Bermuda wedding was Thomas's surprise destination gift to his wife of three months. All the couple's close friends and family were flown in, and a Thanksgiving feast was held for all their guests at the resort the day before the ceremony.

The guests sat on chairs draped in white linen and tied with hibiscus pink and orange organza sashes, while their bare feet rested on the island's famous pink sand. Simone's hibiscus bouquet was inspired by the same colors. Her sleeveless blush-colored charmeuse gown was trimmed with rose gold beading, and Thomas wore a tailored tan wedding suit and turquoise tie that matched the Bermuda waters.

Carly, who now wore a large engagement ring, tried to comfort little Kendrick while his uncle Martin held him in his arms. James and Alistair were the groomsmen. James, who was also the best man, stood with his hand on his son's shoulders; little Colin was the ring bearer and was very happy to have an important job in his uncle's wedding. Nikki and Becky were the bridesmaids, with Marcy serving as the maid of honor.

Mr. Lemmings, whom the couple had invited to take their wedding photos, was happily snapping away. Simone had convinced Thomas that it would be good to permit Lemmings to display positive photos of his life for a change, and their arrangement allowed Lemmings to sell approved photos of their wedding pictures to the media.

Thomas's grandmother and mother stood with the rest of the family, crying tears of joy. His mother's tears were of happiness and regret. She regretted the things she'd said to her new daughter-in-law, who'd forgiven her when she apologized for her actions. And though her relationship with her son would never be the same, the mother of the groom was happy to see that her Thomas was beaming with bliss during the ceremony.

After giving away his daughter in marriage, Robert Mills sat next to his ex-wife and held her hand as she joined the others who were crying tears of joy.

Later in the day, after the wedding photos, dinner, and cake cutting, Simone and Thomas had their first dance as husband and wife. As the guests watched on, Thomas whispered in Simone's ear, "I've been waiting such a long time for this day, don't plan on getting much sleep tonight."

"Well, you'll just have to control yourself because I'm not staying up all night," said Simone teasingly.

"You know, I've been reading that Bible you gave me, and it

specifically states that a wife must submit to her husband, and not refuse him," he teased back.

"Are you really up to the book of Ephesians already? You've made good progress in your readings, I'm very impressed. For that you will be duly rewarded tonight—just make sure you can keep up," she teased.

Thomas whispered back, "Be very careful, Mrs. Lloyd. If you keep up this talk, I'll carry you away caveman-style right now in front of everyone." Simone smiled but held her tongue; she had no doubt that Thomas would do just that. After the birth of their child, they'd decided to wait until their ceremony before becoming intimate again, though Thomas had had difficulty keeping his end of the bargain lately. It was a miracle she'd managed to keep him at bay this long into the evening. After the couple's first dance ended, the DJ announced the father-daughter dance. Thomas passed Simone's hand to Mr. Mills as he came to the dance floor.

As they danced, he said, "Well Simi, you're no longer my little girl. You are a mother and a wife. I've never been comfortable with you living alone in a foreign city. I know you are smart, independent, and sensible, yet I still hoped you'd move back to the States one day. But now that I know your husband, and I see the love he and his family have for you, I can relax because I know you are where you're supposed to be."

"Thanks Dad, but I want you to know that I will never stop being your little girl," she said. When the father-daughter dance finished, the DJ invited everyone to get up and dance. Thomas came back to reclaim his wife for the next song. As they danced, Simone looked around at her family; her parents held each other closely while they moved to the slow song. Newly engaged Martin and Carly danced together with little Kendrick in their arms. She couldn't think of a time happier than this; all their friends and family dancing around them.

The resort lighting turned on over the terrace as the Bermuda sun slowly disappeared. The love she felt for her husband was overwhelming yet peaceful at the same time. "Thom? Thank you for this. My heart is filled with so much joy; I don't know how to express it."

Thomas said, "Now you know how I felt when you said yes to marrying me." They kissed until Thomas abruptly ended it and said, "It's time for us to go." He took his wife by the hand as they said their goodbyes. Lemmings requested they pose for last-minute pictures with the Bermuda sunset in the background, then he thanked Thomas and Simone profusely for giving him this opportunity, promising to work on their photos as soon as he was back in London. Simone and Thomas picked up Kendrick and kissed him goodbye. When they handed him back to Martin and Carly, and he began to protest, Simone hesitated to walk away, but before she could retrieve her son to hold him until he fell asleep, Laura walked over to sooth Kendrick's need for a bedtime cuddle.

"Mom, call me if he gives you any trouble," Simone said over her shoulder as Thomas pulled her away from the crowd. When his wife wasn't looking, Thomas got Laura's attention and mouthed the words, "Don't call," as he shook his head no. Laura laughed at her new son-in-law.

The newly remarried couple was driven away from their family to a romantic, secluded beach house on the other side of the island. Thomas had arranged for various foods and refreshments to be there upon their arrival so there would be no reason for them to leave. His plan worked; Mr. & Mrs. Thomas Lloyd remained in their love nest for several days; relieving suppressed passions and loving one another to no end, without reservations.

The End

AFTERWORD

There are a few issues that feedback contacts believe should be addressed or expounded upon. I chose not to expand on these topics in the story because to do so would take the plot in a completely different direction; however, they are important topics to discuss, so I've listed them below.

Marriage between a believer and non-believer

2 Corinthians 6:14 states: *Do not be unequally yoked with unbelievers. For what partnership has righteousness with lawlessness? Or what fellowship has light with darkness?*

Some clergymen will not perform Simone and Thomas' wedding because of the above scripture, and they would be within their right to deny services. Others will officiate the marriage for the sake of the child, or because a couple is already cohabitating, and they can use pre-marital counseling sessions to witness to the unbeliever.

The significance of Laura's Armenian ancestry

The second issue is the mentioning of Laura belonging to an Armenian parent, yet she does not follow the Christian faith.

Armenia, the first nation to adopt Christianity, suffered

greatly for their faith. It's estimated that over one million Armenians were massacred by the Turks during WW1. They were burned, tortured, and forced into a death march out of the Ottoman empire. Armenian women and children were raped and/or forced into the Islamic faith. The Turks feared Christian Armenians would side with their enemy; so, they decided to kill, and expel the Armenian people from their country.

Sexual misconduct between a professor and student

One feedback reviewer stated that since policies are in place to prevent professors from having relations with their students, sexual misconduct hardly happens anymore; but according to collegestats.org, 14% of surveyed students had been sexual with a professor. Most say the relationship was consensual, but no one knows how many of these young adults were, like Simone, groomed for sex without realizing it.

ABOUT THE AUTHOR

Irene Williams is the author of, The Gracie Chronicles, her first novel which was published in 2020. Originally born in Brooklyn, New York, Irene currently resides in the New York City borough of Queens with her husband and daughter. When not writing, she can be found hiking, or working in her organic urban garden.

9 781736 080320